A JAZZY LITTLE MURDER

A Violet Carlyle Mystery

BETH BYERS

SUMMARY

JUNE 1925.

Violet and Jack have returned home from their honeymoon and are back to their old lives. Jack is taking cases again. Violet is writing books with her twin, managing her business interests, and decorating her house.

When their crew of friends gather for a night on the town, they intend to enjoy cocktails, jazz, and maybe a very late dinner. What they don't expect is one of the band to fall dead while they dance. The celebration comes to a stumbling halt, and the group turns their attention—once again—to murder and why someone would kill a member of the band.

CHAPTER ONE

"We can't leave without visiting Dragonera," Violet said, her cheek pressed against Jack's chest.

They were lying in bed with the doors to the balcony open. With the wind coming in off of the sea and the call of the gulls, it was a near perfect moment. Should she have cared to sit up, she'd have been able to look out and see the crystal blue waters of Formentera Island. Instead, however, she was curled up on her new husband's chest.

"It's just an empty island, love," Jack said, his fingers tracing along her spine. "Before we leave Spain, there are a lot more exciting places to visit."

"It's called *Dragonera*, and we're here. We must. The name alone begs a visit. I might even need to write a little pulp novel about dragons who live there. Surely if anywhere has dragons, it's there?"

"With a princess and the knight who saves her?"

Violet laughed and shook her head. "About the princess who saves herself, you silly creature. She'll make friends with the dragon and fly around the world."

"Ah, of course." Jack laughed, winding their fingers together. Violet turned onto her stomach, placing her chin on his chest to stare up at him.

He was quite a bit larger than her, a mountain of a man really with broad shoulders, a thick chest, and quite strong arms. His gaze was dark and nearly all-seeing above those rugged features she loved so much.

She wasn't a small woman, though she was also not large. Of a middling size with fine, sharp features, dark hair and eyes, and a willowy frame well-suited to the style of the day. Against Jack's chest, however, she felt a little bit like a fairy creature. She smiled a wicked grin that warned him she was about to tease.

He beat her to it. "You're ready to go home, I think."

Violet pressed a kiss to his chest before she shot back, "*You* spent the afternoon drinking coffee with that policía."

Jack's expression was a little self-deprecating, but he only shrugged in reply.

"I might miss my twin," Violet admitted as she laid her cheek back down on his chest. "And writing."

"And Denny, Lila, Isolde, Rita, shopping with your friends, teasing your brother, and generally causing mayhem and disorder."

Violet gasped, lifting her face up again with a fierce reply. "Ham, cigars with Victor in the garden, working, Indian food in the afternoon, just general Englishman-ness. Spain is too hot and too ah—emotional."

"Now we're making up words?" Jack demanded, but she

could see the twitch in his lips and knew that he was no more upset than she.

She laid her face back down, admitting to herself that she was ready to go home. "Maybe we should visit Dragonera, visit Madrid—"

"You've a list of Spanish alcohol to buy, haven't you?"

Violet tried an innocent hmmm, but he tickled her until she confessed. "Yes, yes. I have a whole list of things that Victor requested, along with a few others. We must buy it all for him and for us."

"Anís is—"

"A must for Victor," Violet smirked. "You have never been so sick as you were after an evening of that one."

Jack sat up, pulling her along with him, as she laughed at his remembered pain. He admitted, "It packs a bit of a punch."

"It knocked you off your feet and through the whole of the next day," Violet reminded him. She jumped out of bed and ran for the bath. If they were leaving the warm, beautiful waters of Spain, she needed to overindulge in swimming so it would be a little less painful to leave the crystal seas behind.

She put on her knit swimming costume and then a cover-up. When she left the bath, Jack had already changed into his own swimwear, and they hurried down to the beach, diving into the sea.

Later that day, Vi's wish of learning to tango showed what a brilliant mind she possessed, she thought, as Jack bent her down over his arm. She grinned up at him and wrapped her leg around his. There was just *something* about Spanish music. Especially at the end of the day, with candles burning along the edge of a dance floor that opened onto the beach.

She'd spent nearly every morning swimming, and nearly every evening dancing. The night air filtered in and as the dance ended, Vi pulled Jack onto the beach with her.

"Are you sure you're ready?" Jack asked, dropping a kiss on her forehead. She dumped her shoes on the sand and hurried to place her toes in the water.

"No," she admitted. "Dance the tango with me in England?"

"Always," Jack promised as he rolled up the cuffs of his evening pants and followed her into the water. "We should really have warm beaches in England and all would be well with the world."

"Stiffen your upper lip, good sir." Vi laughed as she twirled in the water, splashing him with her toes. "Englishmen don't quibble at freezing water."

The light of challenge appeared in Jack's gaze, and Vi shook her head frantically. She turned to run, but he caught her about the waist and lifted her, legs kicking. He turned her as though she were a doll and held her protesting over the water.

"Are you sure you want to play this game?"

Violet tried a pout but it didn't work.

"Come now, my love," she said, trying and failing to get away. "Falling into the ocean on our final night before Madrid is no way to end things." She fluttered her lashes, but he scowled.

With a laugh, she wrapped her legs around his waist and told him, "You'll have to peel me off or go down into the water with me."

The expression on his face at her dare was all the warning

she got before he dropped back into the water, dousing them both.

A week later as their steamship approached London, the dark skies threatened them with a downpour that would pause anyone but a Londoner. Violet was wearing Wellingtons, a raincoat, and a smile.

"I can't wait," Violet said, breathing deeply. "There's something perfect about the smell of rain."

Jack settled his chin on the top of Violet's head and mmmed. They watched the dock near as the ship came in, knowing they'd leave their luggage to the servants and hurry home. Violet wanted to go straight to Victor's house, but it was midnight.

Yes, she thought, she should definitely appear at his door. She grinned at Jack when she heard him give the cab driver Victor's address. Jack hadn't even asked. Her knee was bouncing as they made their way through London.

"Why is it taking so long?"

The cabbie glanced back, but Jack just waved him back to the road. Violet rubbed her lip as she watched the blurry road pass by. It was taking too long, she thought. She had been sad when she was leaving behind the warm waters of Spain, but now...goodness, she wanted to throw herself at her twin and also Kate and also tease him and also hear all the stories of what had happened while they were gone and also tell him all of her stories.

When they turned onto the street where Victor's house

was, with Vi and Jack's only a few doors down, she started to scoot towards the door. Jack stopped her.

"Wait until the auto stops, Vi," Jack said calmly, and she glanced at him, grinning in the darkness. She couldn't see his expression, but she didn't need to see it to know it was long-suffering.

The auto rolled to a stop and Jack moved out of Vi's way. She crawled over him and out the door to run up the steps to Victor's house. While Jack laughed and paid the cabbie, Violet banged the door-knocker until Victor opened the door.

"Violet, you lost devil you." He looked her over with matching dark eyes and grinned at her with a matching elfin grin before sweeping her up into his arms. They had a near-silent conversation, eyeing the other for the tell-tale signs of either happiness or stress.

Victor stepped back inside with her in his arms, kicking the door shut behind him, and twirled her in a circle as he demanded, "Where have you been all my life?"

Violet rolled her eyes and grabbed his cheeks, pinching them. Jack let himself into the house as Violet said, "All your life? Mostly right next to you, brother mine. Where is Kate?"

"She's sleeping. She fell asleep in the parlor waiting for you to appear and didn't wake when I carried her up the stairs. Violet Junior, minx that she is, has been kicking in the middle of the night and waking poor Kate."

"Put her down," Jack ordered Victor, "and make me a cocktail."

"Something hot!" Violet added, grinning at poor Hargreaves who appeared in the great hall. "Hargreaves, my friend, how nice to see you. I'm sorry we've arrived so late."

"It's good to see you've returned, my lady," Hargreaves replied, shaking off her apology. "I'll bring hot coffee and tea."

Vi followed Victor into the parlor, wishing she could run up the stairs to her bedroom and change her clothes, but her clothes were two houses down. Somehow coming home had felt like coming here, but she didn't think it was the house or the location of her things. It was simply the location of her twin.

"I have missed you," Violet told him. "The islands were, however, amazing. You should go. We should go back! I'm already ready to go back. I feel the need to go swimming again."

Victor laughed and handed a coffee mixed with something chocolatey to Violet and another to Jack. Then Victor dropped onto the Chesterfield next to Violet. "Did you learn to tango?"

"Yes! You should do it when Kate can move freely again."

Victor smirked, glancing over his shoulder at Jack. "What about a swimming pool for your house, Jack. What do you think?"

"I think!" Violet declared. "I think very much. Can we make this swimming pool somehow an island as well? With sand. A beach? A distant band playing music to dance to in the waves?"

"I suppose we could," Jack said. "Without the distant band and such. A swimming pool would certainly be possible."

"Yes," Victor declared. "You do it."

"Maybe at the country house. We do need to go and update it, Vi," Jack said after a yawn. "You haven't even been yet, Vi. It reeks of my mother and grandmother. Father just handed it over, you know? I think you were dancing with Victor when Father handed me the keys officially. We should update things. Maybe take a weekend trip and send the fellow down who did the house here."

Violet lifted her brow and then leaned back. "You know, we should start with a swimming pool there and then consider one for the London house. There's more room for a swimming pool, right? I can't believe we've somehow missed spending time near the country house."

Jack leaned back with a yawn. "Whatever you want, Vi."

"You've trained him already!" Victor snorted. "I expected even Violet to struggle for at least half a year."

CHAPTER TWO

"I found a dance club with tangos," Jack told Violet three days later. She was lying in bed with her dog, Rouge, sprawled on her chest. Rouge was gazing into Violet's gaze, licking Vi's chin and then whining under her breath. The little dog snuggled closer, and laid her face between Vi's cheek and shoulder.

"I think Rouge is sad," Violet told Jack, tilting her head backwards to look at him from the bed. "I think she misses Victor's Gin."

"Are you trying to say you want another puppy?"

"Maybe." Violet grinned at Jack, still upside down. "Is that a yes?"

Jack snorted and leaned down to drop a kiss on Violet's forehead. "It is, indeed, a yes. Ham telephoned."

Violet's mouth twisted, knowing Jack would be taking a case and their holiday would end.

"I'm not going to leave London quite yet, Vi. They only need a little local help. I verified that already."

"It's not like I don't have books to write and friends to have lunch with." She winked at him from upside-down still, and he shook his head at her. She could, however, see the twitch at the corner of his mouth that said he found her both ridiculous and charming. She considered that the perfect combination to Jack's usual staidness.

"Save some of those lunches for me." He pressed another kiss on her upside-down face, and she could feel his smile when she started to giggle. Rouge mmphed, and Violet felt the dog shift to frantically kiss Jack's cheek as he straightened. With a final goodbye, he left their bedroom.

Before rising from the bed, Violet turned Rouge onto her back and rubbed her belly until the dog's whining stopped. She moseyed to the tub and drew herself a bath, adding oils and salts, and then settled into the water. She was, she supposed, delaying doing the things she usually did. She'd only seen Kate and Victor since their return, but there was a family dinner that evening at Vi's own house.

The family dinner was actually only going to include Ham—Jack's best friend—as well as Violet's friends, Rita, Lila, and Denny, and, of course, Violet's twin, with his wife, Kate. Jack's father had been invited, but he declined in favor of a fortnight at a hunting lodge with some of his cronies, while Violet's own father and stepmother hadn't been invited at all. Vi winced a little at the idea of leaving her father out, but she wasn't ready for her stepmother.

She dunked herself under the water and worked soap into her hair as she debated whether or not she wanted to feel guilty. She decided against feeling guilty and allowed herself the freedom of not wanting to deal with her stepmother.

Violet hadn't hired a new maid now that her previous maid, Beatrice, had become Violet's assistant and secretary, and she was still debating whether she wanted to hire another as she dressed. She chose a comfortable, lightweight day dress and then made her way from her shared bedroom with Jack to the office boudoir.

Her typewriter was covered and there was a stack of paper standing next to it. She stared at it for a while, then threw herself onto the chaise lounge and picked up the newest Edgar Rice Burroughs novel. Violet snuggled down and read until she lost all track of time and Jack knocked on the door of her office.

"Got a lot of work done today?"

Violet blinked stupidly at him, trying to snap back into the world she knew and out of her book. "None," she answered finally. He grinned at her unapologetic reply and she asked, "You?"

"Ham and I had lunch."

"And cigars."

He nodded, the corners of his lips twitching.

"Did you even talk about the case? Or you did, but it doesn't feel like working because you love it?"

"That last version." This time he actually smiled. Rouge, lying at Violet's feet, had her tail flapping frantically, but she was too comfortable to greet him with anything more.

Violet laughed at him. Together they dressed for dinner. When she arrived in her parlor, she circled it. The last of the furniture had arrived while they were gone, and she wasn't quite used to the space. She was still taking it in when their guests arrived.

"How many chalkboards did you buy?" Denny asked as he joined her. He kissed Vi on the cheek. "Missed you, love. Lila was woebegone."

Lila rolled her eyes. "Denny moped. Victor isn't nearly as entertaining as you are, love. My poor lad made me read him detective novels."

Denny nodded as Victor started mixing cocktails. "I want one of those chocolate ones." Denny grinned at Violet with a bit of a smirk, and she prepared herself for a joke. "I," he said, raising his voice to something of an announcer level, "am Watson. You are Holmes. Jack is Lestrade."

"Objection," Victor inserted. "I think Lila and I are Watson—in combination—and me more than Lila. Sorry, love."

"Forgiven," Lila said dryly, accepting her cocktail from Victor. "I prefer to be whoever is lounging in the back with the cocktail, watching the show unfold."

Victor winked at Lila. "Vi can be Holmes, but Jack is clearly Irene Adler. You, Denny, are Mrs. Hudson."

Violet took her chocolate cocktail with a sigh. "I think Holmes is a bit much. Jack is the famous detective, not I."

"As do I," Jack replied evenly. "Of the two of us, Violet is far more likely to commit a crime. I believe she is Adler and I am Holmes."

Violet snickered as Victor's expression admitted that Jack was accurate enough about the more criminal of them.

"So," Victor suggested, "if Jack is Holmes, Violet is Adler, who is Watson?"

"Violet can also be Watson," Jack said.

"No, no, no," Denny declared, "this doesn't work at all. I'm sorry, Jack, but Violet is the more interesting detective. Being willing to break the laws is my favorite part about her."

"You are making me sound like I go around causing mayhem. I am, generally, nice and kind."

"You bullied Gertrude into confessing, so your wedding wouldn't be delayed. You set her up, lied to her, and made sure Scotland Yard was listening."

Violet grinned. "I did do that, didn't I?" She sniffed and then sipped her cocktail. "It was deserved."

"It might have been," Denny agreed. "The key thing here is that *I'm* Watson."

Violet reached out and patted Denny's hand. "I don't mind if you're Watson, Denny."

"Oh laddie," Lila laughed, "if they made a mocking version of Holmes, you could be Watson then. Stumbling through an investigation and barely surviving some Machiavellian villain by sheer happenstance."

"Are you saying I'm stupid?" Denny demanded.

"Mmm, more lazy," Lila told him. "Now refill my cocktail, please."

Denny shot her a look, but he rose to get her cocktail glass and handed it to Victor before flopping back onto the sofa. "It's hard to be me." He pouted towards Vi and then said, with a complete change in attitude, "Saw Jack at the club. He said you're looking for a place to tango. I know one."

"Do you?" Violet asked as their butler appeared in the doorway to announce Ham and Rita.

"Know a fellow who works at the tango club. The bloke's a bit dramatic." Denny nudged Violet and waggled his brows towards Ham and Rita appearing at the same time. "Tends to have a story that's full of rumors and secrets."

"They don't sound very secret," Rita said as she took a seat next to Vi, kissing her cheek and then accepting a cocktail from Victor. "If he's just blabbing them all."

"You'd think so. But he only tells little bits of the story here and there. You never know if you have all the pieces. No one knows but him. Sometimes I'm not sure if he knows at all or if his own half-stories become the truth in his head."

"Oooh," Violet said, lifting a brow at Denny. "That sounds a little poisonous, my friend. Why do you like this fellow who works at the tango club?"

"He's almost as fun as you, Vi." Denny laughed at the look on Vi's face and added, "You're not poisonous, my friend. I don't like him so much, now that I think about it, but he does throw a good party."

"Why don't we eat before Denny offends Violet and refuses him entrance to the house?"

"Speaking of leaving Denny out," Violet said, pausing long enough for Denny to squirm, "shopping tomorrow, ladies?"

"Never," Kate said. "Have fun, dolls. I will never approach a shop again ever. I'm just going to wear sackcloth and ashes, mourning my figure and my wardrobe."

Violet only laughed at Kate's whine. There was little doubt in Vi's mind that Kate's poor swollen feet were the issue, not her shape. Violet had witnessed her sister-in-law running her hand over the baby bulge too many times with a soft look on her face.

"Uh-oh," Vi said, "Victor didn't rush in to tell you you're beautiful growing the baby."

"He's only allowed to say it once per day. He's trying to give me a fat head, I think. To go with my fat feet and my fat stomach."

Vi groaned and nudged Victor. He kept his mouth shut, but she could read his thoughts in his gaze and laughed at the combination of panic, stress, and frustration.

"Stop it," Victor told Violet.

Her expression told him that she'd never stop, but she reached out and took his hand, squeezing. "I wrote some of a new book."

"Good," Victor sighed. "I've gotten stuck on about three. My writing process includes you telling me all the things I'm doing wrong. When I know it's off, I find myself just thinking, I need to talk to my Vi." Victor glanced at Jack to watch him react and then smiled to himself when Jack lifted a silent brow.

Ham, however, laughed while Rita tried to hide her reaction. The butler saved both Jack and Victor from pretending to fight and they made their way to dinner. Dinner was delicious, as was the conversation. When they finished, Denny said, "Well, loves, we could go lay about the parlor, listen to the wireless, and enjoy our people being back where they belong."

"Or?" Jack asked.

"The fellow I know is playing at a new little club I also happen to know. It won't be tangoing this time, but it should be fun all the same."

"Never," Kate declared, pointing to her feet. "Victor will go with you. I'm going home to loll about, beached-whale style."

"We can just stay here," Violet told Kate, hooking their arms.

"Darling Violet," Kate said, patting her cheek, "don't be silly. I want to loll about with you or without you."

"I'm certain I ordered a lolling lounge."

Kate just grinned and shook her head. "I need my bed, darling one, but I will loll on your sofa soon."

CHAPTER THREE

The club was slightly larger than a hole in the wall with a nest full of chipmunks fighting for space inside. There was an actual line out of the club, but Denny led the way to the person standing at the door, whispered something in his ear, and pressed something into his hand. A moment later, the door opened and they were led inside.

"This feels illegal," Ham remarked, glancing about and pulling Rita into his side as a drunk young man nearly stumbled into her.

"It probably is," Denny agreed happily. "Fun, however."

The dance floor was crowded, there was a bar along one wall with people fighting to reach the barman, the smoke was thick in the air, and beyond the scent of too many bodies pressed together was the smell of mold and mildew. Violet scrunched her nose but then the music started with the wail of a trumpet. She paused and turned and Denny shouted, "See!"

She did see. Or hear, rather. It was as if an angel were playing the instrument.

"Oh," Violet breathed. Jack tugged her into the center of the dance floor. Given his size, the press of bodies on the floor didn't overwhelm them. They danced until sweat was pouring off of both of them and Vi forgot all about the crowd, the smoke and the mildew.

When the band took a break, Violet and Jack did as well, looking about for their friends. Vi could see nothing above the crowd, but Jack took her hand and led them through the throng. Victor was leaning back with a cocktail, and Violet immediately stole it from him before glancing around. Denny and Lila were chatting with the trumpeter from the band while Ham and Rita were in line for cocktails. Jack jerked his head towards the bar and left her with Victor.

"Meet Joshie Barnes, Vi," Denny shouted above the din. "This is the girl I was telling you about," he said to Joshie.

"The witty one?" Joshie turned towards Violet and gave her a charming, lascivious grin. He held out a hand that was strong and calloused from his instrument. His skin was a bit darker, and Violet wouldn't have been surprised to find that the man in front of her had an interesting genealogy. His dark eyes raked over her, and she found herself flushing at the way his gaze lingered on her chest and then moved on to her legs. Her evening gown was rather short, and she hadn't considered that until this Joshie fellow made her feel about one breath from naked.

When his gaze returned to hers, she lifted a brow, and he didn't even look the smallest amount ashamed. Violet turned to Denny and lifted the same brow, and he—at the least— blushed slightly and shrugged as if to say: what can you do?

Violet sipped Victor's cocktail and then suggested, "Perhaps we should try to find some fresher air?"

"This way," Joshie said.

Violet glanced at her brother. "Can you see Jack?"

Victor nodded. "They can see us."

Violet followed Denny and Lila who followed Joshie. They moved through the crowd towards the back of the building and ended up passing a roomful of people half-hidden in a thick smoke that wasn't quite right. Violet scowled when she noticed one young woman sleeping with her mouth open and legs spread.

"Just a moment," Violet said, leaving her brother and crossing to the girl. She pulled the girl to her feet and heard a, "What?"

"Time to go home, love," Violet told her.

"Oh, no. I need my fellow to take me home. He stepped out. He'll be back soon, I'm sure."

Violet's smile belied her anger. "I have a driver. I'm sure one of these gents would tell your fellow that you've gone."

"Oh." The girl blinked slowly, and Violet was sure the girl was more than just tired and zozzled. Vi wanted to track her beau down and give him a piece of her mind, but instead, she took the girl towards the exit with Jack pacing beside her.

"This place is something Denny would find," Jack said as he helped bring the girl to their auto and sent her home with their man. "It's horrible."

"And fabulous," Violet admitted as the auto drove away. She breathed deeply. "The air is so much fresher, isn't it? After that club?"

"Violet," Jack replied with a baffled glance, "I am almost certain I smell urine."

Vi grinned at him and wrapped her arms around his neck. "Perhaps just a little. The club, however, was rank in a way that demands a thorough scrubbing and possibly burning our clothes."

Jack pressed a kiss against her forehead. "You're right. You are foul now."

Vi gasped and shoved away, but he tangled their fingers together.

"I adore you still."

"My feelings are under debate after such a comment as that!"

"It was no good of that fellow to leave his girl like that." Jack sighed, but it was more of an angry sound than an unhappy one. "She could so easily have been harmed. Whoever the man is, I'd like to teach him the error of his ways."

Violet laughed, stepping aside what looked like a bag of trash that had been torn apart by feral dogs. "I am not certain I am wearing the right shoes for this place."

"Certainly not," Jack agreed, wrapping his arm around her waist and lifting her enough off the ground that her shoes weren't destroyed.

"What a useful gent you are. A rescuer of shoes, a carrying of burdens—even me—a...ah...something very gallant indeed."

"Is this *my* Vi struggling for words?" Jack side-stepped the line and walked to the front. The bloke at the door clearly wanted another tip, but Jack told him. "We're only playing once for entering such a place."

"Mebbe I won't let ya enter," the fellow said, straining a rather prodigious neck.

"Maybe I'll report this fire hazard to the authorities and have you shut down," Jack suggested idly as though discussing the weather. "Come now. You know we've paid once already."

"Bobby ain't gonna like you sent his girl home," the fellow said.

"Then perhaps Bobby shouldn't have left her to herself in such a state," Violet snapped. "He's lucky all we did is send her home and not off to a convent. She surely needs someone to intervene."

"Bobby don't like mouthy dames," the fellow said, giving her something of an evil glance, as though this Bobby would be able to teach her a woman's place.

Violet winked at the doorman just to watch his ears turn red. A moment later, he cursed and opened the door to the club, letting Violet and Jack back in.

"You should turn them in," Violet told Jack.

"Feeling vengeful, sweet Vi?"

Violet scowled at the press of bodies and yelled over the clamor. "I suppose we must at least tell the others before we leave them to be poisoned by the air and drinks here."

That time, they had to push through the crowd despite the lateness of the hour and the size of Jack. The band had begun again but without Joshie, and it had none of the brilliance it possessed with him.

Violet could almost see the appeal of this place. It felt exclusive, like only those who knew about it would find it. It catered to music lovers with the band and the forbidden with what had to be drugs. The man at the door only letting in people as he chose, it made others feel left out. It made their own forbidden trip—when it happened—feel all the more like something special. In the end, however, she'd prefer Indian food with Jack or dancing on the beach.

"This place is ridiculous," Violet said as she passed a woman whose dress had flipped up in the back. They'd entered the hall with the slew of back rooms and were pausing in each doorway as Jack glanced in to look for their friends. Violet paused at the sight of a woman fervently kissing a man against quite a dirty wall. Her dress had slid up, and Violet snapped it back into place before telling Jack, "I want to go back to Spain. Why can't we just be taken there as if on angel's wings?"

"Shall we leave in the morning?"

Violet almost nodded to see if she said yes whether he'd pack a bag that evening and buy them tickets on the next ship, but she knew that Victor would never take Kate this close to giving birth to their baby. She sighed and shook her head. "I can't leave Victor and Kate and the baby, and there is no way that Kate will go. Perhaps we can get her to motor down to the country house with us? We could take it slow and easy and get her there to have the baby in their new home. That would be better than London, surely? We could horseback ride and breathe country air and—"

"Get the stink of this place off of us," Jack agreed. "I think we'd need to take Lila and Denny or he may weep right into his coffee every morning without you."

"Darling Jack, is that jealousy I hear?"

"I am almost entirely certain Denny looks on you as his personal performing monkey."

Violet choked on the sudden shock of laughter just as they heard shouting from behind another door. "Shall we make a wager?"

But Jack wasn't listening, his head turned to the door. "Certainly that is Victor."

Violet paused and realized it *was* her twin. He so rarely got furious to that level. She'd just assumed her friends had somehow involved themselves in whatever dramatic things were happening in the back rooms but this was something far, far more serious.

Jack opened the door, and Violet's jaw dropped as she saw Victor shaking Martha, Lila's sister. The girl was dressed so scantily that Violet felt like she was wearing a nun's habit by comparison.

"Are you trying to ruin my life? What is the matter with you? Bloody hell, woman!"

"Victor, old man," Denny said easily, "perhaps don't knock her teeth out of her head."

Lila was watching Martha be shaken like a rag doll, easily balancing her drink. She sipped idly from it as Martha's wailing head rolled about her shoulders.

Victor didn't even pause in his tirade until Violet shouted, "Victor Ulysses Carlyle, let go of the girl at once!"

Victor turned, his cheeks and ears red with fury and his lips covered in lipstick.

"Oh heavens," Violet said with a gasp, "it's on his collar. I will slaughter her myself." She started forward just as Jack hooked his arm around her waist.

"I believe," he said calmly, "that there are enough witnesses to protect Victor from getting in trouble. Especially when we make him scrub down at our house to get the stench of this place off of himself. I believe those with child tend to have more sensitive noses."

Violet glanced at Jack and then at Victor, who was still in

a rage with his fingers digging into Martha's arms. "Darling," Violet told Victor, placing her hand on his wrist. "You're leaving marks."

"I find I care little."

"Regardless," Violet snapped, shrugging off Jack's hold, "let her go. Kate will be fine. She knows you adore her."

"But why?" Martha demanded. "The plain little thing, completely unstylish, so bookish."

Victor shoved Martha away from him, but not before Violet gave her a ringing slap. Martha gaped in horror as Violet slapped the loose girl once again. "Do not play games with my brother's happiness, you idiotic child."

Martha let a crocodile tear loose, but her calculating gaze met Violet's in challenge.

"Don't think you'll win against me," Violet told her flatly. "There's little I wouldn't do to ensure you lose."

Martha dropped her hand from her face and straightened her dress. "Lila, what kind of sister are you? You didn't do anything to help me."

"If I have told you once, I've at least told you twice," Lila said idly, "you're making your own bed. If you are determined to paddle your way to hell, I'm not going to waste my energy trying to row you back."

Martha stamped her foot and then glanced about. Joshie was smoking in the corner of the room, an open grin on his face at the scene, while another man scowled at all of them. Rita and Ham were nowhere to be seen. Violet felt a flash of worry at the recollection that Rita was something of an adventurer and Ham was a former soldier and now a Yard man.

"I hear you're the one who floated my girl away," the other man told Violet.

"What are the chances," she asked Jack, ignoring the man, so she didn't turn into a crazy fishwife on him, "that the auto is back?"

"Small."

"Indian food?"

"What time is it?" Denny asked. "I'm suddenly hungry. Has it been so long since we ate?"

"Hours," Lila answered. "It's nearly morning. I'm surprised you haven't noticed."

"Must be why I'm so famished."

"Indian food," Jack agreed. "Victor, find Ham. I'm taking the ladies out of here. Did you want to bring along Martha?"

"She's hardly a lady," Lila answered, and Martha scowled at her.

"I suppose we must," Denny sighed, taking Lila's hand and placing it on the crook of his elbow and then taking Martha by the upper arm in what looked to be a not so gentle grip.

CHAPTER FOUR

"Is this goat?" Lila demanded with a sneer, shoving her plate away. "Denny!"

Denny giggled and Violet was sure he'd purposefully ordered his wife that meal.

"Goat?" Martha gasped. "Goat?" She stared down at her plate.

"Oooh," Rita said, tucking a loose curl behind her ear. "Yum." She reached out with a fork and took a bite. "Oh, that's so nicely spicy. My nose is burning."

"Do you like your nose to burn?" Denny asked, staring down at his plate and then taking the naan. "At least they have this weird flat bread. By the sweat of your brow and all that."

"Denny," Violet said and Victor finished, "You've never worked by the sweat of your brow."

Jack leaned back and ate his food next to Ham. Ham's gaze was fixed on Rita, who was happily eating the spicy goat dish. Violet smiled at the sight. She had to wonder whether Rita realized Ham's interest and if she was avoiding it. They did seem a little like pals, but if Ham wasn't half in love with Rita, Violet would eat her hat. Speaking of, she rather wished she had worn one. It was nearly morning, and the only people eating at this hour were a few night workers glancing at Vi and her friends and the other spoiled crowd in evening gowns and suits, as though they were birds of paradise inexplicably found on a Scottish moor.

"Why were you in the club, Martha?" Violet asked the girl, who had her arms crossed over her chest. She was pouting like a child and every time she tried to turn her whining gaze on Victor, Violet was tempted to slap the girl again.

"I was the one who told Denny about it," Martha snapped. "He found the roving club, got the passwords, all of it, from me. I'd tell you that you were welcome, but I clearly regret my choices."

"So do we all," Lila said idly. "You are completely out of control, and that is coming from Denny and me, who don't actually care."

"If you don't care then why am I here?"

Lila's sneer had Violet choking back a laugh as her best friend explained. "Because, foolish one, when Father finds out that I knew you were there and left you, it's my fault. If I drag you out, write to him, and then wash my hands of it, it's his fault or yours, but I'm clear."

"You are diabolical," Violet told Lila.

"It's why you love me," she replied, and the two friends grinned.

Violet handed her a samosa. "I think you'll like this."

Lila took it dubiously and risked a careful bite. She finished it rather reluctantly and then declared, "Where is the auto? I want to sleep before the sun rises. Maybe then my body will forgive me for this food and those cocktails."

"They were bad," Violet agreed.

"Of course they were. It isn't about the best of everything," Martha said snidely. "It's about being authentic."

"Authentic?" Violet let her disgust color her voice.

"Feeling, experiencing, interacting, like the human animals we are."

Violet slowly drew in a breath to allow herself a moment to think before she replied. "Those you were spending time with were certainly animals. Leaving a girl in the state we found her. You attacking Victor with your lipstick."

"Don't speak of it." Victor's eyes sparked with anger once more.

"You were the one who lashed out," Martha snapped, eyes flashing but with much less effect than Victor's glare. "You two think you're so much better than us because your father is an earl."

"Only better than you," Violet said brightly, "but not because our father is an earl. None of us would have left another as defenseless as Joshie's friend left that girl. None of us would have left her like that."

"So you interfered," Martha sneered. "Stuck your noble nose in. She needed to be there. Bobby isn't going to be kind to her because you took her off."

"She needs to leave him, then," Violet said simply.

"We're not all as fortunate as you, *Lady* Vi." Martha looked triumphant, as though she'd won the argument.

Denny cleared his throat. "*You* have been, however, little

Martha. Maybe your Joshie could wax poetic about his work ethic with his job at the tango club, for your roving criminal clubs, and at private parties, but you can't. You have a closet full of clothes your daddy bought you, your pockets full of ready money your daddy gave you, and your entrance to nearly wherever you want to go because of the connections your family provides you."

"Just because Daddy gives me money doesn't mean I'm not trying to live an authentic life." Martha sniffed and rolled her eyes as though the rest of them were fools.

"What is it," Rita asked idly, "that makes something authentic? Surely this food is authentic. Perhaps the experience in this restaurant? Or walking down a street? Those are all *authentic* things."

"It's not *pretending*. It's the struggle, the dirt...the grit of it all. The sweat of your brow like Denny said, but *real*. The animal needs of your body. The...the..."

Denny scoffed, and Lila yawned at her sister before lazily saying to her, "Do shut up."

Martha's mouth snapped shut but it didn't stay closed. "You see what I mean," she said to Rita.

Rita straightened. "There is something invigorating about the experiences that go with survival, but I suspect that you're romanticizing them."

Martha pouted as Rita continued. "It is just as authentic to admit you're spoiled and enjoy the fruits of your parents' labors. Authenticity is about being genuine. Surely throwing yourself in with another crowd and romanticizing their authentic struggle is condescending. Your friends seem to be struggling in reality to survive. And you, at any time, have only to hold out your hand for a step up. Are they even your friends or just enjoying what you can do for them?"

Martha's pout had deepened to a full, furious frown, but Rita ignored it.

"I have traveled with tribes in Africa and seen their wildlife. I have ridden a camel and sat by a fire and eaten snake and goat and turtle in a wilderness. As enjoyable as I found my journey, I am no more authentically any of those peoples nor would I pretend to have their knowledge."

"Don't you see our knowledge as superior?" Denny asked quizzically.

Rita laughed at Denny. "Ours? Over theirs? It would depend, wouldn't it, on our location."

Denny stared at Rita. "Whether Africa or London, you're still fluent in languages they've never even heard of."

"But in Africa," Ham told Denny, "we are the infants and they the wise men. I am certain that in some savanna—we would die in days."

"If not hours," Rita agreed.

"Whereas in London? They might need our knowledge to survive just like we'd need theirs to survive in Africa."

The look on Martha's face soured as she became more and more entrenched in her pout. Especially when Rita finished her lecture. "You are doing the equivalent of pretending to be a tribesman when you've really been raised in the countryside of England. There's nothing wrong with making friends across all races and stations. I think the quibble point comes when you romanticize the struggles of another without understanding them. None of us here truly know what it is like to worry about being able to buy enough food, but your friends just might. None of us know what it's like to give birth in a hut with a dirt floor, but pretending it's more real than the way you might give birth—that's not fair to their struggle."

"Speaking of giving birth," Victor said, "I'm off to your house, Vi, to scrub the filth of tonight off of me"—he shot Martha a venomous look—"and then to go tell Kate of the night. If she throws me out, I'll be on your doorstep woebegone and alone when you return."

Violet rubbed her brother's back. "Kate is irrational right now. Perhaps carry a shield to fend off whatever shoe she throws at you."

"Just tell her the truth," Lila said, "but start with how much you adore her."

"I've been put on a budget of those as well."

"Did you want me to come with you?" Violet asked, knowing he did.

He gave her his best spaniel's gaze and she rose, Jack rising next to her. "May we see you home, Rita? Or Ham?"

"I'd be happy to," Ham said. "I believe we'll be passing your house, Denny?"

They left the restaurant and Violet watched Jack stop and thank the staff and then let him tuck her into his side. It was coming on warmer days, but at that time of night or morning or however they wanted to view it, there was a distinct chill in the air.

Their driver had located them, though he'd had to buy their location from the man at the club door despite Denny already paying the fellow to see them home.

"Did she get home okay, Jimmy?" Vi asked.

Their driver nodded. "No trouble at all, ma'am. Except she seemed rather surprised to find herself at her parents' house. I think she wasn't quite—ah—well. I asked her for her home address and took her there, but she was confused when we arrived. Her mother about wept into my shirt, ma'am. Then her father carried her inside and the two of them were crying on each other while I was trying to wriggle out and get back to you."

"Oh my." Violet glanced towards Jack but the auto was dark at that time of night, so she just murmured, "I hope that it turns out as well as it can."

"It's hard to say, isn't it?" Victor's tone conveyed the same thoughts that were edging about Violet's mind. If they'd been brought in that state to Aunt Agatha, they'd have been cried over and then scolded and probably sent off. If they'd been brought in that state to Lady Eleanor, she'd have only cried while Father was present and then she'd probably have tried to beat them senseless for the shame of it all.

"Hopefully her parents are like Aunt Agatha," Violet said for them both.

"Indeed," Victor added. After a moment he asked, "Jack, what would have happened to you if you'd turned up on your parents' doorstep in such a state?"

"My father probably would have hugged me until I couldn't breathe, shaken me until I begged him to stop, and then dragged me off to some carefully planned recovery."

Violet had yet to know her father-in-law very well, and she couldn't quite imagine the kind man shaking Jack at all. They were clearly father and son, their looks and sizes similar.

"By Jove, Vi!" Victor cried. "What will I do if I get a wart like Martha? Who knows what Kate is brewing? Maybe it's a devil!"

"Certainly it is," Violet said agreeably.

Victor moaned as Violet laughed at him, running her hand over the top of his head. He was clutching it between his hands, though she could only see the shadow of him.

"Darling Victor," Violet said seriously, "just ask yourself what Aunt Agatha would do."

He shuddered a moment later and repeated, "What would Aunt Agatha do? Yes. That will work. My God, what I wouldn't give for her to be here. To help with the baby. To talk to her. What if I muddle him up?"

"You won't," Violet said.

"Hah! Says you. No one likes me more than you, Vi. Not even Kate."

"You're a good man, Victor. You'll do your best, and it'll be enough."

Victor clutched Violet's hand in the dark, sitting slowly up. "What would Aunt Agatha do? Bloody hell, I'm a maudlin fool at this time of night. We're not so bright and so young anymore, Vi. It's time to turn in a bit earlier."

"Midnight?"

Victor scoffed. "Don't be ridiculous. Perhaps before 3:00 a.m."

CHAPTER FIVE

"It's all your fault," Martha told Violet the next morning. Martha's arms were crossed over her chest and she seemed to be on the edge of stomping her foot. "Lila sent a telegram to Father, and he's coming to drag me home."

Violet sipped her Turkish coffee slowly and then set her teacup back on the saucer. "I hardly think that has anything to do with me."

"Lila told me last night you'd have done the same for your sister."

"Write a telegram? I suppose I might have."

"She's just tattling. It's like that time I broke her doll."

"You did that on purpose," Lila told Martha, taking up her own teacup. "You always were spoilt."

"You're still getting revenge for it!" Martha shouted, stamping her foot. "You've always hated me and want me to suffer."

"Only some," Lila said idly. "It's good for your soul."

"You're just jealous that Cousin Godfrey left me more money than you."

Lila sighed and took a deeper gulp from her coffee cup. "Save me, Violet. Do you have a muzzle or a gag?"

Violet shook her head and then looked up as Jack stepped into the room. Her dog, who was sitting at Violet's feet, picked up her head and barked once. A small wriggling red and white creature yipped back. Violet's mouth dropped open and she jumped up just as Jack dropped down to kiss her. They collided and somehow, Jack maneuvered himself into her chair with her on his lap and the pup in her arms.

"Oh!" Violet cooed. "Oh!"

"I believe you requested one of these," Jack said as Violet kissed the little dog on his head. He licked her nose, tail wagging so hard it was providing a steady metronome beat to the moment.

"What a display!" Martha gasped in feigned shock.

Jack stiffened under Violet, but she leaned in and kissed him on the cheek.

"You can pick another, if you'd like," Jack said. "This one was the favorite of the mother's owner. Said he was the sweetest of the lot."

"Hmph!" Martha's tone was patronizing and completely devoid of any recollection of how they'd found her last night, dressed as she'd been.

"Do shut up," Lila told her sister.

"Do," Violet agreed. She rose and pulled Jack to his feet, nudging him towards the Chesterfield and took a seat at his side rather than on his lap. Rouge leapt up onto the couch next to them and stuck her little black nose towards the puppy. The pup wriggled frantically but Rouge bypassed the puppy for Jack's lap.

"Victor stopped by once he got up," Jack told Violet, playing with her fingers with one hand while he scratched Rouge's ear with the other. "He's decided that we need to go to the country houses until the baby arrives. He wants you to come, but he's determined to set out by the end of the week. He said, and I quote, 'Aunt Agatha often talked about the importance of clean air for children.'"

Violet's lips twitched. "I suppose some time in the country would be agreeable. Lila, you and Denny will come with us?"

Lila nodded. "Denny is becoming a bit soft again. He's like a half-baked bun, too soft in the middle. Jack, you'll have to walk him."

"Like a dog?" Jack asked.

"Just so."

"I'd like to help Ham finish this case," Jack told Violet.

She paused and then nodded. She wasn't quite ready to be separated from Victor again, but they'd follow soon after. "I do need to do some shopping. We should send that same clerk down again to see what needs to be updated at the house."

"Good idea," Jack said, dropping another kiss on her temple.

Martha huffed like an offended Victorian grandmother, and Violet was tempted to slap the girl again.

"Back to it," Jack said, kissing her on the lips this time, and Violet noted the twitching edges of his mouth that declared he'd done it as much to irritate Martha as to steal a moment of affection with Vi.

Violet laughed and leaned back. "Thank you for the puppy."

"Seemed fated," Jack told her off-handedly. "You wanted one. I heard tell of one. Just the thing."

"Perfect," Lila said. "I'll foist the baggage off on Father, we'll shop, and then we'll take the pups down to the country with our newest things. Violet, did you see the orange dress with the gold overlay that Harriet Anderson was wearing the other night at the Savoy?"

"It was perfection," Violet agreed as Jack backed away.

"I'm not going to put up with this treatment," Martha announced, setting her teacup down and standing.

Lila sniffed and in her idlest voice said, "If you think I won't knock you down and drag you back into this parlor by your hair, please recall when you did break my doll."

Martha stared at Lila, who slowly lifted a brow.

"You can't make me do what you want."

"What I want," Lila told Martha, "is for you to take the trouble you're determined to throw yourself into away from me. I have little doubt that you're determined to ruin your life, but if you think—even for one moment—that I'll spend the rest of my life listening to Mother bemoaning that I didn't keep a close enough eye on you, you have forgotten what I am capable of."

Violet blinked at the sheer, cold nastiness in Lila's voice and watched in shock as Lila sipped her coffee again before she added calmly, "Do sit down, dear, you're blocking the view."

Martha dropped onto the sofa. Violet closed her mouth and went back to petting her dogs.

"Paris?" Violet asked Lila.

"Too close," Lila said. "There's too much of a chance that they'd expect me to jaunt over and pick her up."

"New York City?" Violet suggested, lifting a brow at Martha.

"Are you talking about where I might go?" She sounded aghast.

"Talk to Rita. She can suggest somewhere far away," Violet told Martha, "but still fun. Be authentic somewhere else if you must."

"Why do I have to leave?"

"Because you aren't without family," Violet said. "If your mother is really going to blame Lila, it's the least you can do."

"But I don't want to," Martha whined.

"You can't be all that attached to your friends here."

Martha paused.

"Foreign men are more exotic," Violet added. "I've met many. I would lay a wager that Rita could tell stories that would make your hair curl in the best of ways." Violet spoke to Martha as though she were describing a new chocolate treat to Denny—enticingly with a sort of longing tone.

Martha sniffed, but Violet could tell by the brightness of her eyes that she was interested. "Rita will help you find the right place," Violet told her. "Somewhere truly *adventurous,* but you'll need to be good before we leave. Hands and lips off Victor, don't even speak to Kate, and stop antagonizing Jack."

"I want to say goodbye to my friends. They're playing at that tango club tonight and then at one of our roving parties."

Violet met Lila's gaze. Her friend shrugged slightly.

The fellows from the club the night before had certainly been neglectful of their friend, and there had been some shady activities happening the corners. Violet had little doubt that there would be drug users at the party. If they kept an eye on Martha and then turned her over, maybe she really would seek adventure elsewhere?

"You could stop walking the edges of society and experimenting so much and stay here."

Martha scoffed.

"Midnight scavenger hunts, bottle parties at the baths, boating, those things are fun without being out and out stupid."

As soon as Violet said stupid, she knew she'd ruined any chance of Martha remaining. Her face screwed up. "You all think you're so smart with your spoiled lives and your idiotic playing. Scavenger hunts?" The snide tone carried across the room. "I don't think so. I'll put up with your control, I'll go home with Father, and when I leave, I'll consider Rita's suggestions, but sooner or later Father won't be able to control me."

"Father can't control you now," Lila said in her casual way. "If you were willing to actually work and scrap and struggle like your friends, that would be different. Doesn't Joshie work three or four regular jobs?"

Martha blushed deeply before she sniffed dismissively. "Don't be stupid."

Lila ignored her sister and sipped her coffee again. "Did Kate give Victor any trouble?"

"Happily, she wasn't all that surprised. Victor does whine very compellingly as well, so that helps. She softened up with his pleading and somehow he got her to take him off his budget of compliments and loving."

"I'll go home with Father and not give him any trouble," Martha broke in, "if you tell him that your friend suggested I see more of the world."

"Father isn't going to let you gallivant about by yourself."

"I'll handle that part," Martha said.

Lila shrugged. "Whatever it takes to get you out of my hair would be lovely."

"You don't have to act like I'm lice. You're always so mean and then act surprised when I make my own friends."

Lila completely ignored her sister and asked Violet, "In the country, what will we do?"

"Badminton?"

"No," Lila said.

"Tennis?"

"No."

"Horseback riding?"

"Perhaps once or twice," Lila conceded.

"Sleep late, listen to the wireless, read novels, possibly have the gents row us about on the lake?"

"Better," Lila sighed. "I do want to read the next Holmes novel. Also, we picked up some of those Edgar Allan Poe detective stories. I like those. And his creepy little tales. They're my favorite, but they give Denny nightmares."

"Of course they do." Violet laughed.

"He woke up screaming about the beating heart the other night. I had to rub his back until he fell asleep."

Violet laughed until she cried and when she finally gained control of herself Martha demanded, "The tango club *then* the party after. I want to see them both places."

"As long as you behave." Lila yawned. "Oh, I can't wait until you go away. You make my head hurt and make me feel as though I'm eleven years old again."

"I hate you!" Martha shouted.

"If we had to have a sister around," Lila told Violet, "I don't see why it couldn't be Isolde. Isolde doesn't whine. She has good taste in clothes now that she imitates you. And Tomas is all right, too."

"Isolde only imitates Violet because Tomas is in love with Vi," Martha said meanly. "Everyone knows that."

"Does everyone know what it feels like to have their ears boxed?" Lila asked as she popped a petit four in her mouth.

"It's the truth."

"It's false," Violet told Martha evenly, trying to imitate Jack. "And it's cruel. If we wanted to be mean and cruel, we'd mention that your lipstick is on your teeth, your dress doesn't fit properly and it's whorish, and we'd tell all the awkward tales of your childhood to everyone we meet. We don't have to be nice to you, Martha. We're trying, but if you keep pushing, you're going to discover we've run out of patience and tolerance."

CHAPTER SIX

The tango club was in the ballroom of a hotel that had branched into a restaurant, dancing, and rooms. Violet supposed that they'd be able to pour some of their overindulged customers from the bar area into one of their hotel rooms should it be necessary, a handy arrangement for all involved.

Vi wore a red dress that dipped low in between her breasts and flared around her calves with zig-zag shapes that drew attention when she danced. Her shoes had heels and diamond buckles, and were strapped about her ankle. With her black pearls, her diamond bangles, and a pearl and diamond headpiece from Jack with her bobbed hair curled under it, she was confident she would shine on the dance floor.

"They have professional men and woman to dance with you if you don't know how to tango," Martha said, all of her earlier venom gone. She looked excited, and Violet didn't blame her. This ballroom was filled with excellent music and twirling bodies. It begged to be joined in, and Violet had little doubt she and Jack would be back time and again.

"Do you know the professional dancers?"

Martha nodded. "They're some of my friends. Some of the band from last night, who can't play instruments for the tango music. Most of the band works here too. As barmen or waiters or coat check. Bobby's girl, Heather, is a coat check girl. Sally works as a dancer. Henry—he plays the bass—plays with the band here. Joshie is in the band, too, but plays bandoneon. He's so good too. I doubt you'll have heard anyone who makes it so...enticing."

"Perhaps not," Jack said kindly as though he were trying to not be irritated with the girl.

She was, Violet supposed, rather young. Violet suspected that the girl was half in love with one of the men, but she wasn't quite sure which one. Vi didn't even care. Maybe she should be more charitable than she was, but she was struggling for even the most basic tolerance. Jack held out his hand to Violet and they turned back towards the friends, winking as they swung into the dance with ease.

"When does the father arrive?" Jack asked, moving with Violet through the dance.

"Not soon enough," she said, loving the feel of his hand on her while they danced. Any woman could fall in love while dancing, but she felt certain that dancing with the man you loved was the best way to stay in love. Especially a dance that required so much cooperation and attention to the other. How could she not love Jack when she felt his eyes on her face, his hands on her body, the way he moved with her, held her as though she were a treasure, and all because she'd expressed a wish to tango.

"That Martha is an interesting one." Jack leaned Violet over his arm and then let his lips run along her chin. "I'm not sure you can trust her agreement to be good."

"I don't," Violet admitted through the trembles his closeness still caused along her skin. "Lila doesn't either."

Jack snorted and they slipped back into the dance without talking. The music continued, and they moved to it as though they were communicating by touch alone. Violet and Jack only left the dance floor when the room had become so hot that they needed a cocktail.

"I would like a lemon ice," Violet told Jack, knowing it was impossible. "It's so hot in here."

"That does sound perfect," Jack agreed. "The housekeeper when I was a child would make those on the hot summer days. I always felt like the luckiest little fellow."

Violet grinned at him. "Surely not little."

Jack's grin was a little self-deprecating as he admitted, "Perhaps not little. I suppose I was a bit of a monster then as well."

Violet laughed as they moved towards the bar together. She kept one hand on Jack's arm and her gaze on the dance floor, trusting him to lead her without letting her bash into anyone. Denny was flushed and irritated on the dance floor, dancing with one of the professional dancers. The girl looked a little familiar, and Violet suspected she must have seen Denny's partner at the party the night before. Despite the way Denny was stumbling through the dance, the look on the girl's face was pleasant. Violet would love to have been near enough to check the look in the girl's gaze.

"Poor Denny," Violet laughed. She smirked up at Jack and then looked for Lila. She found her friend at one of the tables bordering the dance hall, sipping from a cocktail with a second cocktail in front of her.

It was a pity that Rita and Ham hadn't come with them to the tango hall. Rita, it seemed, could already tango, but she did want to see the *authentic* roving dance party, so she intended on meeting them before the evening was over. Violet wanted Ham to come too. She had created this fairy-tale in her mind where Ham and Rita fell for each other, but they seemed more like buddies, with Ham being particularly attentive.

Vi glanced up at Jack. "Do you think Ham cares for Rita?"

Jack looked down at Violet with that infuriatingly elusive grin twitching at the edge of his mouth. "What do you mean?"

Violet's scathing expression had Jack grinning, but he didn't answer her question. She huffed, let go of his arm, and left him for Lila. A few steps away, Violet paused and said over her shoulder, "I want something with ice and something sweet."

Jack lifted a brow and Violet rolled her eyes at him and then walked the edges of the dance floor. Martha was dancing with the fellow named Bobby who had left his girl so defenseless. Violet scowled at the duo and saw that Martha —at least—caught Violet's expression.

Violet arched her brow at the girl and then smirked coldly enough so Martha knew what Vi thought of her part-ner. She flopped down next to Lila.

"My feet hurt." Violet examined Lila's two cocktails and then took one of the drinks from her.

"Darling, I fought for that drink."

"Jack's bringing more," Vi said, refusing to give up the stolen cocktail. "Denny looks as though he might weep."

Lila laughed but then her expression changed as she nodded behind Violet. Martha had approached with the Bobby fellow on her arm.

"Looking for my girl," Bobby said, belligerently. "She didn't show up tonight or last night."

"Hmmm," Violet said, pretending she didn't know. "I sent her home."

"She didn't arrive," Bobby snapped. As he spoke, the girl and Denny approached the table and then Jack with a waiter and several cocktails.

"I'm sorry to hear that," Violet lied.

"What did you do with her?"

"Put her in the auto. She gave her address. The driver took her home."

"She didn't get there," Bobby snapped. He moved forward to loom over Violet, not knowing that Jack was just behind him.

"Ah," Violet told Bobby. "Interesting."

"Interesting?" Bobby demanded. "What happened to her?"

Violet sipped her cocktail and told him honestly. "We asked her for her address. The driver took her to the address she provided. Perhaps she didn't want to return to you?"

Bobby's gaze narrowed, and he started to reach for Vi, but Jack took hold of the back of Bobby's neck with one hand.

"I don't mean to be unkind," Violet told him, knowing she was lying again, "but if I were your girl, I would not have returned to you either after the state I found her in."

Bobby flushed, gaze narrowing, but Jack's massive hand kept Bobby from doing anything other than scowling at Violet. He took in a deep breath. "Please. I love her."

The girl with Denny started and Martha cast Bobby a dark look.

"I don't mean to be cruel," Violet lied again, "but leaving your girl like that is not love."

Bobby's expression was cold with anger. "I love her."

As if saying it over and over again would make Violet tell him where she was. "Bobby," Violet told him gently. "She's safe. She knows where you live. She'll return to you either when she's feeling better, or she's decided that she doesn't want to return."

"You can't do that. You can't just interfere."

"All I did," Violet told him, "was help her to an auto and send her home. Anything since then has been her choices. It's not like you're married, right?"

Bobby flushed and glanced away.

"Of course they aren't married," the girl with Denny said. "What a ridiculous thought. She's your—" Whatever the girl was going to say Bobby cut off.

"Be quiet, Sally. It's none of your business." There was enough emphasis on business that Violet wondered just what the girl had been supposed to be doing.

Martha laughed nervously. "Bobby, darling, Heather is just your assistant. She's not your girl."

"Do you think you are?" Bobby laughed meanly. "The

spoiled princess from the north? You bring in the swells. That's all."

Martha's gaze widened and her eyes filled, but she blinked whatever she was feeling away so quickly, Bobby didn't even notice.

"Calm down, Bobby," Sally said. "We're working. Put on a smile. We'll find Heather. She told you she wanted to get married, didn't she?" Something in Sally's tone suggested she wasn't too keen on that idea.

"I'm going to find her," Bobby told Violet. "I'll marry her and you won't be able to take her away again."

Violet took another sip of her cocktail. "I would say good luck to you, but I honestly don't care what happens to you."

"Then why won't you tell me where Heather is?"

"I don't believe in making other girls' choices for them. She knows where you are. If she wants to find you—well..." Violet didn't bother to fill in the rest. Honestly, she thought, the girl had given the driver her home address. Her parents had taken her inside and wept over her. Violet suspected that Bobby had been keeping Heather from her parents. Perhaps her parents had spent the day begging her to stay with them.

Violet couldn't be sure.

"Bobby." Sally laughed woodenly. "It's just Heather. She's just another rich girl slumming. Sooner or later she'd have left you. We'd all heard of that gent who wanted to marry her. She'll do it eventually and have a kid or two and pretend that we never happened."

"Nah." Bobby shook his head. "Nah. She loves me. I know she does."

"That doesn't mean she's going to stay with you. And do what?" Sally sneered. "Have your babies in some abandoned warehouse where we have those parties? She's not our kind any more than Princess is," Sally said with a sneering glance at Martha.

Martha's jaw firmed and she swallowed thickly, but Violet wanted to pat her on the back for the bright expression on her face. Her gaze was narrowed and cold, but her overall expression said she wasn't bothered at all.

"Excuse me," Denny cut in a little too giddily. "Please clarify. Princess is Martha."

Sally shot Denny a look that said he was an idiot.

"Lovely, I see. Heather is the girl Violet took out of the party last night and sent home. Bobby here is the arranger of these events. Sally is clearly in love with Bobby, biding her time for the man to look up and see her."

Sally scoffed and hissed, "Get back to work, Bobby. We're all going to be let go and then where will you find your next round of spoilt lovers?" Sally spun and hurried off.

Denny took the seat next to Lila. "Thought that might do it."

Jack let go of Bobby's neck. "Stay away from my wife."

Violet's lips twitched at the order and Lila oohed. Denny giggled happily while Bobby snapped, "Tell her to keep away from my girl."

"As Violet said, your girl knows where you are. Now get out of here." Jack handed Martha a drink and held out a chair for her before taking the final seat. "What a drama. I felt as though I was reading one of Violet's favorite books."

"I do like them ridiculous."

Martha sniffed over her drink, and Violet could see the girl was struggling for composure.

"Tangoing is hard," Denny told the others. "The drinks are good, so I suppose we could come back."

"Violet and I will be back," Jack said idly. "The music is excellent. As you said, the cocktails are good."

"Tangoing is provocative," Lila said. "I feel certain someone turned over in their grave the moment we started dancing it."

"It's fun," Violet said with her wickedest grin.

Lila met Violet's gaze and they both grinned. "Bobby is handsy. The other gent barely dances better than Denny. I would like to learn with someone capable. Jack?"

"No," Denny said. "You've already identified him as Holmes and me as Mrs. Hudson. I'll learn and then I'll teach you."

"Jealous?" Lila asked idly.

Denny's answer was to reach out and take hold of Lila, pulling her in for a resounding kiss. As he let her go, Martha groaned. "Even the smallest of towns would be better than seeing you lot moon over each other."

CHAPTER SEVEN

"*L*adies?" Violet asked as she finished her cocktail.

Lila nodded and rose and Martha sighed and came too. They made their way around the dance floor to a back hall, and as they started down the hall, Violet paused. "It's dark, isn't it?"

"Perhaps a light blew?" Lila said idly. "I do wish to use the facilities, however, and I need to fix my lipstick after Denny ruined it."

"Do you really think they don't like me because I'm rich?" Martha asked in the darkness as though the cover could hide her emotions.

"Yes," Lila said flatly. "If they cared about you, they wouldn't have said what they did in front of you. Did you already say goodbye?"

Martha sniffed a little watery. "I told Bobby I was leaving but I wanted to return soon. He didn't seem to care. When I said something to Sally right after we got here, all she wanted me to do was not tell Bobby where Heather was. I didn't even realize Sally had feelings for Bobby until Sally started talking about Heather stepping between them and putting on a brave face. I—"

"Did you give him money?" Lila asked flatly.

"Once or twice," Martha admitted as they found the door to the ladies. "He just needed a little boost, and it was easy for me."

"I'm not saying couples don't share money," Lila told Martha as she turned on the bathroom light. "They do. Denny gave me money often before we married. Father kept me on a tight leash because he didn't want me marrying Denny. Now, we share all we have."

"What about you?" Martha asked Violet.

She considered before speaking. "Look, Jack has money. He's never needed anything like that from me, and he's old-fashioned enough to never ask me. Even if he wasn't, it's not fair to compare two well-off folks to what you and Bobby were."

"Rich men are...spoiled and think they...." Martha stopped in frustration.

"I know," Violet told Martha flatly. "Lila doesn't know because she was married to Denny in her head since she was seven and a half, and Denny loved her even longer. Do you have any idea how many rich or well-connected fellows thought I was theirs for the taking? Seeing my father or the possibility of whatever inheritance I might receive? And then after I did inherit? By Jove! It was raining money-grubbers even after I was engaged to Jack."

"How am I supposed to find someone who loves me if the rich men don't and the poor men don't?"

"Don't start with their pocketbook," Lila said. "Denny inherited *after* we were married."

"What do I start with?" Martha demanded.

Violet glanced at Lila, noting the shock on Lila's face. It was easy to see the sisters had never had a heart to heart conversation.

"Their character. How they treat you. How they treat the people around them. How they treat staff. Think of the people we know. Victor, Jack, Ham, they're all generally kind."

"They don't count," Martha said. "They're all taken."

Violet wasn't going to argue with Martha. Instead she said, "Aunt Agatha told me once that ridding oneself of a husband was a difficult endeavor. It's far better to choose wisely."

"But how?" Martha demanded.

"Stop being stupid," Lila told her sister lazily. "You knew Bobby was no good. Did you not see that Heather girl overcome by drugs and alcohol and left alone in the way she had been?"

"She shouldn't have taken them," Martha shot back.

"She shouldn't have," Violet and Lila agreed in unison with Lila continuing, "But *he* wasn't overcome by drugs. True love doesn't leave your lover alone. Not like that. What if that had been you? What if it wasn't *Violet* who stepped in but some...some...criminal? Heather was lucky. Maybe she didn't turn up here tonight because she realized how lucky she had been?"

"Is she really all right?" Martha asked.

It suddenly struck Violet that Martha hadn't cared before that moment. Perhaps she had trusted it would all work out, but Violet would have tracked Lila down and ensured she was well. That's what friends did.

"Of course she is," Lila said with disgust, as if she'd realized the same thing that Violet had.

They each separated to take care of their needs and met back at the mirror to freshen perfume, powder, and lipstick. Violet ran a comb through her hair and then rearranged her headpiece and straightened her jewelry.

"You're pretty spoiled," Martha said with her gaze fixed on Violet's diamond and black pearl choker that was surrounded by the long strand of black pearls Victor had given her. Between Jack and Victor, Violet had quite the collection of pearls and diamonds.

"I am," Violet agreed. "Victor spoiled me before Jack did and to be honest, I've spoiled myself on occasion." She held up her diamond bangles before winking at Martha in the mirror. The conversation in the ladies had taken a turn for the serious, and Violet very much wanted to return to Jack's arms and set aside Martha's problems.

As she left the ladies room, Martha called, "I'm just going to talk to Sally."

Violet glanced at Lila who shrugged. After Martha left, Violet hopped up onto the table with the mirror. She sighed and took a deep breath in. "Your sister is a mess."

"I know," Lila said. "I suppose we should go back, but I am enjoying not having Martha around. I feel like a bad sister."

"You are one," Violet told Lila.

She smiled lazily. "I suppose I am."

"She's a bad one too," Violet told Lila.

The light in the hall was still out as they left the ladies, and there was a loud crash. Violet gasped and stepped back into Lila, who steadied her. Someone appeared in the hallway. Violet knew immediately it was Jack from his build.

"Vi?"

"Here." Her voice was bright enough to allay his worries.

"What's wrong with the light?"

"We couldn't find it, so we followed Martha to the ladies." Violet started towards Jack and there was another crash. She took Lila's wrist and hurried forward

"Martha went the other way," Lila sighed. "Probably to throw herself at that Bobby fellow."

"The band is on a break," Jack told them, looking into the darkness, but none of them could see anything. "Joshie came over to talk to Denny and knew immediately that Heather had returned home. He'd been trying to persuade her to do it and seemed relieved. It seems Joshie is another of the slumming ones. His father is a barrister or something. Joshie asked that we keep her location quiet. Give her a chance to straighten out, he said."

Violet sighed. "The stupid things girls do for love or their version of it. Martha is there chasing down that noise because she thinks she loves that Bobby fellow."

Joshie appeared in the darkness a few moment later with Martha. He was pulling her protesting behind him.

"You'll see," Martha hissed to Joshie. "Heather will appear at the party later. She loves him as much as I do. Not that it matters." Martha dropped a tear, but it was so calculated and perfect, Violet felt sure the girl could cry on command.

"Stop it," Joshie snapped. "I've got seven sisters. I know what fake tears look like, and I'm unpersuaded even by real tears. Why would I feel bad for you crying over Bobby? You know what he is even if you don't want to admit it."

"What is he?" Violet asked Joshie.

He shook his head.

"What happened?" Jack asked.

"A tiff between Bobby and the management. Bobby is in a right mood and it's coming across with his partners. They're not all like Martha, willing to pay for his meanness."

Martha flushed and tugged herself away from Joshie.

"Everything's all right?" Jack asked again.

"Yeah." Joshie sighed. "Maybe I should go work for my father. Bobby puts together well-paying jobs, but he's a snake. I feel like the man who got bit by a cobra when he picked it up. I knew what he was, and I still let him into my life."

"Don't," Jack told Violet as she opened her mouth to somehow offer rescuing him. Truthfully, she didn't know how to rescue the man, she was simply inclined to try. "He can take care of himself."

Lila took Violet's arm, twining them together. "Are we dancing more?"

"I've lost a bit of the flavor of it tonight," Violet admitted. "Maybe we should go back to the house?"

Violet didn't care one way or the other. She had wanted to spend the evening with Victor, but he was hovering over Kate, who did look a little green about the gills, Violet had to admit. With Kate's swollen feet and constant look of having just had bad shellfish, Violet was certain she wanted to wait for a while to have a baby of her own. Either way, Victor was hovering, Violet missed him, and Jack was distracted by the thoughts of his case.

"I want to say goodbye to Heather too," Martha said belligerently. "I'm sure she'll be at the party tonight."

Violet lifted a brow in question at Lila, who sighed. "I suppose we did promise. Father is to arrive tomorrow. Shall we indulge her this last time?"

"Yes, but then we're going to plot out a mystery story with Denny. I need something to do once Victor takes Kate to the country and Jack finishes his case."

"Why don't you simply nap and shop?"

"She's not you," Rita laughed as she joined them. "Did I miss all the fun? You have that expression that says your bed sounds lovely."

"Martha is pouting." Lila yawned and glanced towards the table where Denny seemed to be napping. "It has poisoned the evening."

Martha gasped as Joshie stepped away, nodding once at Rita.

"Did Ham come?" Rita asked, taking Lila's free arm.

"He was called to Lyme by our superiors," Jack answered.

Rita smiled, but Violet felt certain she was seeing disappointment in the woman's eyes.

"You want to go to the party tonight. Don't you, Rita?" Vi asked.

The blonde nodded. "Distract me, please. My feet are itchy, and I have a desire to disappear to Siam."

"Siam?" Martha demanded. "Why?"

"Why not?" Rita returned. She grinned at the others and then shrugged. It seemed to be impossible to convey why she loved to travel, only that she did.

"May I go with you?" Martha asked suddenly. "Do you travel alone or with friends?"

Rita looked taken aback. "Some friends of mine are going at the end of the week."

"At the end of the week?" Violet gasped.

"It won't be forever," Rita replied easily. "Shall I bring you something amazing?"

"Yes," Lila answered immediately.

"What about Ham?" Violet demanded, regretting it instantly.

Rita's gaze seemed to be veiled, but she shrugged again. "I would love a G&T." She was clearly changing the subject.

Jack took that as an excuse to pull himself and Joshie away.

"Father won't let you go to Siam," Lila told Martha, but her sister didn't respond.

"Siam?" Violet asked Rita, feeling a little bit of a whine in her voice. "Why don't you wait and go to Cuba with us?"

"You aren't going to Cuba until after Kate both has that baby and recovers," Rita told Violet. "My feet are itchy now. I'll be back before you go to Cuba, I'm sure. I'd love to go when you do."

There was another crash from down the hall and then Bobby came storming out of the darkness, dragging Sally behind him. He threw her towards the others. "I never loved you, Sal. Never will. I'll find Heather and make her marry me."

"You just heard about the money her grandmother is supposed to leave her. It won't make you a rich man. Heather said it wasn't much."

"I said I loved her."

"You don't love anyone but yourself. You think Heather

can draw you from the gutter? She can't. You're trash. You always have been, and you always will be."

Bobby stared at Sally and then, in a sudden strike, slapped her hard.

Their shouting had the manager of the tango club rushing over. "Quiet! Quiet!" He tried a nervous smile for Violet and her friends. "My apologies. My deepest apologies. Please believe me it *isn't like this here, normally.*" To Sally and Bobby, the manager said, "Out with you! Out! By heaven, this behavior is intolerable."

Sally was already in tears, holding her face, and she ran to the back of the tango hall. Martha stared after Sally and then looked aghast at Bobby.

He turned to Violet, leaning in to speak in a threatening tone. "You'll be telling me where I can find Heather."

The manager gasped and shoved Bobby back. "Leave her be."

Bobby lifted a brow and said low and even, "I'll be seeing you."

CHAPTER EIGHT

"He said what?" Jack asked. His voice was a near growl and his shoulder had tensed, making him look like an enraged bear.

"I'll be seeing you," Rita replied, voice low and evil. She had squinted her eyes and hunched up a little as though Bobby had been imitating a witch when he'd threatened Violet. Vi shook her head. She'd have thought better of Rita, but then again, Violet had irritated her friend with that question about Ham.

"To Violet?"

"With an evil gaze," Rita agreed.

"He was just angry," Violet laughed. "Embarrassed and upset at being dismissed. Nothing to worry about."

"It was a little concerning," Lila told Jack, curling her hair around her finger. "If Violet were anyone else, she'd have shuddered and gasped. Maybe wept a little."

"I've never heard him talk to anyone like that," Martha

said, shivering. She rubbed her hands down her arms and then threw back the last of her cocktail.

"See," Lila said, pointing at Martha, "like that. Violet is too cool-headed to be scared of Bobby, but anyone else would have been flinching at the way he spoke."

"I'll be seeing you?" Jack's voice was the one that had everyone else pausing. He sounded too much like a demon from the depths of hell.

"Oh ho," Denny said, clapping Jack on the shoulder. "It's not like he knows where you live. Vi'll be fine."

"It's not like *Lady Vi* is hard to find," Jack snapped back. His jaw was clenching and releasing, and his eyes were cold and hard.

"Calm down," Violet suggested lightly. It was the wrong thing to say.

"We aren't waiting for him to come at you when I'm not around, Vi," Jack told her. "We'll go to this party, and he'll be educated about whether he wants to lay eyes on you again. I assure you, he does not."

"Ooooh," Denny said, rubbing his hands together. "I'll back you up, old man. Not with my, you know, hands. I easily bruise. You should see the mark on my leg from Lila kicking me the other day, but I'll be there to watch. For certain. A witness, you know, that you left him alive."

Violet sighed as Jack rose. He straightened his coat and then handed her up. "Did you want me to take you home first?"

She shook her head and then eyed the others. "You're all coming. There will be no question about whether we left this man alive. Consider it our last hurrah. We're done with these secret parties after this. Next it'll only be drunken scavenger hunts through London at 2:00 a.m."

"Ah," Denny said, jumping up and pulling Lila along. "Our leader has spoken. The festivities have come to an end. Nothing but responsible activities from here on."

Even Jack snorted, but they left the tango club, calling for their auto. They piled into the back while Jack told their driver where to go.

"Another one of those places like the last time, sir?"

Jack said yes, and Violet added, "If a fellow asks where you left that girl the other day, keep it mum, please."

"Yes, of course," their man agreed. Violet crawled onto Jack's lap. It was snug in the back of the auto with all of them, not that she truly needed the excuse. It took a good half hour to reach the location this time, and it did seem to be a semi-abandoned warehouse that was one careless match away from destruction.

"This place looks dangerous," Jack told the others. "Stay together. It's probably a bunch of drunken idiots like Denny."

"Useless the lot of us," Denny agreed. "Be careful. You never know when a fool like me will knock you into a pile of refuse or something equally terrible."

Violet snorted while Lila patted his cheek. "I'll keep you safe, love."

Martha shoved out of the auto and approached the man at the door. This location was larger than the last, so there was no reason to keep anyone out. The man looked them over as they approached. "Bobby said to keep you out."

Jack simply held up a large pound note. The man noted it

and opened the door, letting them in. "If he asks, you snuck in the side door."

Jack took Violet's hand, and they hurried through the door. Lila, Denny, Rita, and Martha followed closely. It was only then that Violet realized the club was mostly dark. What lights there were centered on the stage where Joshie was wailing on the trumpet. Near him, Bobby was playing a saxophone.

Violet blinked through the smoke, frowning at the makeshift stage. The girl, Heather, was playing the piano while the trumpet wailed. Violet sighed at the sight of the girl, but at least she looked better. Gone was the mostly unconscious female, and she was, Violet realized, playing beautifully. The only one struggling was Bobby himself.

He hadn't shown any brilliance the last time Violet had seen him play; in fact she hadn't even thought of him again. But now, however, he was abysmally bad. He didn't quite hold the notes long enough, they faded out like he was trying, like he'd run uphill a moment before and hadn't caught his breath yet.

He looked pale, Violet thought, her head tilting as Jack moved forward through the crowd. Most people were dancing, but as the music got worse and worse, the dancers were stopping to stare towards the stage.

Jack reached the edge of the stage when Bobby pulled the saxophone away and looked up. He seemed to be looking right at Vi but not seeing her. It was then that he stumbled forward and fell into Jack.

Vi gasped, letting go of Jack as he caught Bobby. Jack laid him down on the floor.

"I say," Denny said as the other band members rushed forward. "Is he all right?"

Jack stood up a moment later, telling the crowd, "Back up!"

Violet stared at Jack. Or rather Jack's hand. It was dark red.

"Give him some air!" Jack ordered. "Someone open that door, let's get some fresh air in here."

"Jack," Violet said, staring down at Bobby. Their gazes met, and he seemed confused. His eyebrows were pulled together, his breath shuddering.

"Violet, get our driver," Jack said. "Go home with him. I'll take care of this."

"Jack!" Violet said again.

"Vi," Jack said, glancing at her. "He's probably drunk or using the same drugs."

"Jack! Your hand!"

Jack glanced down and noted the blood. He frowned. "What?"

"He's not drunk," Violet told him. "He's hurt."

"Come girl," Rita said, "let's get your auto. He needs a doctor."

Violet paused, saw Jack's nod, and left him with Bobby. Jack wouldn't be able to focus on Bobby if Vi were there. "Go with them, Denny," Jack said. "We'll bring him out if he needs a doctor."

Violet shook her head and took Lila's hand. Martha had dropped to her knees next to Bobby and was gently pushing back his hair. Lila glanced at her sister, but she followed Violet and Rita to the exit. They reached it just as the crowd realized something was wrong enough that the police might be called.

"Is there a telephone?" Violet asked the man.

He laughed at her.

"Your Bobby is hurt."

The man blinked and then shouted, "Everyone out!" A moment later, he booked it towards the edge of the building.

"Ah," Rita said sarcastically before grabbing Violet and Lila and hauling them against the building as the already restless crowd stampeded towards the exit. "Good friends are so hard to find."

"Good help too," Lila added, trying to avoid touching the wall of the warehouse while also trying to avoid those fleeing it.

It took only minutes for the building to empty, and half-drunk idiots were running down the street.

"Does anyone else feel certain some sort of monster is going to step from the shadows?" Lila asked. The silence after the music and the shouting crowd was almost surreal.

"Are you all right, ma'am?" a man asked, his voice alarmingly sudden and loud.

Lila screamed before Violet could tell her driver, Jimmy, that she was fine. "We need your help. There's a man who seems to be injured. I suspect we need to either call for help or take him to a hospital."

"We aren't going to find a telephone around here, ma'am," Jimmy said. "And I'll be dismissed if I leave you here, ma'am."

Violet glanced at him and then back at the shut door. "Pull the auto closer."

Jimmy paused and then shook his head. "I think I must insist you come with me, ma'am."

Violet didn't argue. She followed Jimmy to the area where he'd left the auto and let him seat her in the back with Lila and Rita.

"So much for modern women," Rita muttered.

"It was easier to agree," Violet told Rita. "And the last thing I want is the image of another dead body in my mind."

"Do you think he'll die?" Lila asked. She closed her eyes and shuddered. "Poor, stupid Martha."

"Poor Bobby," Rita added.

"He's not dead yet," Violet said. "I've learned to be cautious. I feel like I'm cursed. Having a party? A dead body in the garden. Having house guests? A bloody murder in the parlor. Going to some disgusting illegal club? We'll see, but I'm not laying a wager on the poor man surviving."

"Well when you put it like that," Rita said, "it makes traveling to Siam seem far less dangerous than going on a picnic with you."

"I've survived this long," Lila told Rita. "I thought you were supposed to be adventurous."

"Not foolhardy, though," Rita said. "You know I'm an only child. I can't leave my father alone."

"Then put Ham out of his misery and give your father a grandchild to adore."

Rita's mouth snapped shut and Lila leaned back. "Speaking of a grandchild, Denny wants to make one. Only I find children terrifying after seeing Kate."

"You should," Rita agreed. "Kate seems to be tortured most of the time. Frankly, if I've ever seen a reason to avoid bedding someone, Kate is it."

"I would have asked my mother, but she's fixated on a grandchild despite the adopted children, so I asked my cousin Lucy. She told me that she'd rather be beaten than have another baby. So, I asked my sister-in-law when she was drunk, and she told me having a baby was like being torn apart from the inside."

Violet felt her stomach turn.

"Then, I asked Harriet Kingsley, you remember her, Vi. Well, Harriet has four children, and she told me that it was the most beautiful experience known to mankind and a privilege."

"She always was stupid," Violet said, remembering the way Kate looked earlier that day.

"Exactly my thought," Lila added. "You remember how she used to chew her hair."

"Did you ask anyone else?" Rita demanded. "Ham wants children."

Violet gasped as Lila smirked. "I knew you liked him."

"I didn't say that, and you will forget it."

"I won't," Lila said. "I will bring it up at inopportune moments. However, yes, I did ask someone else. I've asked about a dozen people. I even made a chart."

"And what does your chart say."

"There's a direct correlation between whether I respect someone and whether they told me if it was horrible."

"None of the people you respect have said anything different," Rita demanded before Violet could.

"One told me that the ends were worth the means but that being thoroughly zozzled was to be suggested if you didn't just sick up while you were having the baby. Then," Lila shuddered and leaned forward to whisper, "she said that while she had the baby she also defecated on herself."

"Oh," Rita and Violet said in unison, shuddering.

The driver choked in the front.

"Never speak of this if you want to continue to be employed," Violet warned him.

He cleared his throat. "Ma'am."

CHAPTER NINE

*J*ack exited with Bobby in his arms a few minutes later. He frowned deeply at the auto before turning to look down the street. Martha was a breath behind him with Denny, Joshie, Heather, and another band member that Violet hadn't met. He'd been playing the bass, and Violet thought he might be named Henry.

"They need the auto," Violet told the ladies.

"Jack is never going to leave you alone in this part of London," Lila said, shooting Rita a glance that said, *can you believe this fool?*

Violet opened the auto door without responding and called, "Jack. Here."

He shook his head.

"Jack, if you don't put him in this auto and take him to the hospital, I will feel guilty for the *rest of my life* if something happens to him."

Jack eyed Violet and she added, "Jimmy will stay with me. As will Rita and Lila and Denny."

"I'll stay with her too," the bassist replied.

They all glanced at him and he said, "I wouldn't leave my girl here either."

"Arguing is taking time," Violet told Jack. "I'm hardly an idiot."

Jack growled at Violet. "If anything happens to you, you'll never hear the end of it."

Violet stepped back. "We'll walk until we find a black cab, we'll meet you at the hospital, let you lay eyes on us to ensure we're fine, and then go home. We'll even all go back to our house."

"I only need to lay eyes on you," Jack said. He studied Jimmy and added, "Keep her safe."

"Of course, sir," Jimmy said.

Violet walked away before Jack lingered over her any longer. In order to allay his fears, she sang, "Marco!"

"Polo," Denny called back.

Vi glanced back and saw Denny take Lila's hand and then Rita grab Lila's free hand. Heather and Henry followed Violet and a moment later Joshie did also. Vi hurried on and heard the quick thump-thump of footsteps that told her Jimmy was chasing her down.

"What do you think, Len? Which way shall we go?"

He looked at her as if she was mad and then pointed to the right.

"Marco," Denny called when he reached them.

"Polo," Vi said, rolling her eyes.

"Doesn't it feel callous to play games while some bloke could be dying?"

"Yes," Heather said, glancing at them. "That tall man said he needed a doctor immediately."

"He's a snake," Violet told Heather. "You should know that given how he left you."

"I know," Heather said, "I told him that tonight was my last night. My parents forgave me. They...they took me back. They said I could come home. He always said they wouldn't."

"You were in pretty bad shape," Violet told her. "You probably scared them."

Heather only nodded. "I—I'm not going to go to the hospital. Joshie, will you see me home?"

"You're all idiots," Violet told them callously. "Letting that Bobby fellow control you. Was Heather's parents' house nice, Jimmy?"

They'd reached a busier street, and Jimmy was trying to wave down a black cab. He glanced back at her and nodded.

"So you thought you'd slum with Bobby without talking to your parents? Without even giving them a chance to throw you away?"

Heather looked away.

Vi turned her attentions on Joshie. "Your father paid for your music lessons, didn't he, Joshie?"

Joshie stared at her in surprise.

"Did he go to your concerts?"

Joshie nodded mutely.

"But not since?"

Joshie hung his head.

"Why don't you just talk to him? Tell him what you love doing and ask him for his help? Give him a chance to help you or turn you away. Have you ever, even once, asked him for his advice?"

Joshie shook his head. "He wants me to be a barrister too."

"He wants you happy and safe and secure for when he isn't here. He's not wrong. Being poor and hungry is terrible even if you have your trumpet. If he educated you and supported you and tried to advise you, he loves you. When was the last time you saw him?"

Joshie glanced at Violet and then away.

Vi rolled her eyes. "So you let Bobby influence your life instead of those who actually want the best for you. Sooner or later, however, your father is going to die, and you'll regret not forming some sort of bridge with him."

"What makes you think you're so smart?"

"I lost my mother," Violet told him flatly. "And two brothers, and my second mother. We always believe there will be time, but there isn't. You can continue as you've been and make regrets or swallow your pride and know you tried."

"Vi," Denny cut in with a horrible glee as he hurried to her, "Bobby was stabbed."

She turned to him just as a black cab pulled up in front of them.

"No, he wasn't," she told Denny in a weak whisper.

"In the back! Jack said he'd been bleeding out slowly."

"He was playing the saxophone and working!"

"He was also on drugs," Joshie said. "He never played sober."

Violet closed her eyes.

"If he had used enough drugs, he might not have realized he'd been hurt."

She breathed in slowly and held her breath.

"Whether or not he dies," Denny added, "someone tried to kill that snake."

"We don't know that," Violet lied, more to herself than her friends. "We don't know what happened."

"Keep telling yourself that, princess," Joshie said.

"That's Lady," Lila told Joshie.

Vi's gaze snapped open as Joshie demanded, "Wait, really?"

"Really," Rita said happily. "Lady Violet, daughter of the earl."

"The earl?" Joshie demanded, gaze wide.

"It doesn't mean anything," Violet snapped.

"Only that she's the closet to an actual princess you'll ever get." Denny's giggle made Violet want to slap him. "Violet, have you met a princess?"

"Oh my heavens," Violet said, pressing her hands to her face. "Please stop."

"Our friend could be dying," the bassist said, shocked.

"We're a bit calloused to death," Lila told him. "People keep dying around us. We're like poison."

"Or a malfunctioning rifle," Rita added.

"I prefer to think of us as the jazz-angel, cocktail-wielding hand of death."

"Please stop," Heather said. "You're joking about someone we care about."

"They're idiots," Martha told Heather.

"That is coming from the girl in love with the man who only wanted her pin money," Lila said in an aside. "And who is wearing that dress, which clearly makes her bottom look big."

"Her bottom does look big in it," Rita agreed. "You'd

think the sales girl would have told her."

"Oh stop!" Martha shouted, getting into the black cab. "This one is going to the hospital."

Heather, Joshie, and Henry got into the black cab. Violet stepped back, rather annoyed at Heather, who had clearly changed her mind about the hospital. Vi didn't want to have anything to do with another murder, or attempted murder in this case. She was going to write only *fictional* cases. She might take what she learned and apply it to less ridiculous stories than she and Victor had been writing.

"Do you think we should go too?" Rita asked.

"No," Violet bit out. "We're going home. I am tired of all this murder and nonsense."

"Of course," Lila said lazily, "I would put Martha at the top of the suspect list. I think we have to at least clear her. Or set one of her friends up as the criminal."

"That sounds fun." Denny pulled his wife into his arms and glanced at Jimmy. "What do you say, Jimmy, would you like to lie to implicate one of those fools?"

"I'm afraid I could only do that for Mr. or Mrs. Wakefield."

"Well, Vi's right there." Denny tilted his head, his grin wicked.

"Vi is not a part of this," Violet declared, wishing for Jack's coat. "Vi wants a hot bath and a hot toddy and my bed."

Jimmy waved down another black cab a moment later and held the door open for Violet and the others before taking a seat in the front.

Lila snuggled into Denny, and Violet felt a flash of irritation. Her Jack was driving the auto to the hospital to take a certainly criminal man for help. Jack's hands were covered in that man's blood, and Violet had little doubt that he'd pursue whatever had happened to Bobby regardless of whether the man lived or died. All she wanted was him to be with her and let someone else take the case.

The journey back to her house seemed to take forever, but when they arrived, she didn't need her butler to tell her that Jack wasn't there. Violet glanced at the others and Lila said, "We're taking our usual room."

Vi glanced at Rita.

"The pink one?"

Vi nodded and then added, "If you'd like. The one at the end is done now too. It has a nice view in the morning."

"I plan on sleeping through the morning," Rita said.

"The pink room then."

Rita ran up the stairs. At the top, she looked back and asked, "Are you going to be able to sleep without Jack?"

Violet's gaze narrowed on Rita. "Will you be able to sleep without Ham?"

Rita's gaze narrowed back and then she shrugged. "I've never had the pleasure."

"I bet you could," Violet said with a smirk. Rita spun on her heel and escaped down the hall. Violet glanced back at her impervious butler. "Don't wait up for Jack."

"Is all well, ma'am?"

"No," Violet sighed. "Near murder, it seems. He'll be back when he's back."

"Do you need anything, ma'am?"

She thought she might need the less impervious gaze of Victor's butler. She scowled at him and then her head tilted. "I'm going to step down to my brother's house."

"Ma'am," the butler said, trying to stop her, but she simply shrugged him off, noted the recently started downpour and then ran through it.

She banged on the door at Victor's house until Hargreaves opened the door.

"My lady," he said, only mostly impervious.

She grinned at him, and patted his cheek. "I need my idiot brother."

"I believe he's abed. Would you like a towel?"

"I would," Violet agreed. She took the towel before running up the stairs. As she toweled her hair, she slammed her fist against Victor's door. He opened it a moment later, staring at her in shock.

"We knock now?"

"We're married now," Violet told him.

He stepped back where Kate was struggling and failing to sit up. Victor crossed to her, hauled her up, and shoved pillows behind Kate's back while Violet kicked off her shoes, took Victor's robe, and climbed into bed next to Kate.

"There's another almost body."

"What does that mean?" Kate asked in surprise.

"He's not dead yet," Victor answered, "but someone tried."

"What Victor said." Violet snuggled into Kate's side. "May I pet Violet Junior?" She didn't wait for an answer and pressed her hand on Kate's belly. Kate took it and moved it so that she could feel the baby kicking.

"She's sassy," Violet told Kate. "She wants to come out and play with me."

"What happened?" Kate asked as Violet pressed back on the baby.

"Lila asked everyone she knows about childbirth."

"Bloody hell, Vi," Victor groaned.

"There's a verse in the Bible about it," Kate told Violet. "It's a little comforting."

"Everything will be fine," Victor said desperately. He sounded as if he was going to vomit. "Everything is going to be just fine."

"Tell us about the almost dead man," Kate said, running her hand through Violet's hair. "You've still got all your shiny things on."

Violet started pulling off her bangles and necklaces, handing them to Victor. "This bloke named Bobby. He was abominable. Someone stabbed him and because he was using drugs, he didn't feel it until he fell off the stage. Jack took him to the hospital."

"Ah," Victor said. "Newly married. New near-murder. Someone doesn't want to lie alone in the dark."

"Be quiet," Kate told Victor, pushing back Violet's hair. "Violet has bad dreams, and who can blame her? I've had them too. Sometimes I still remember Robert Moore and the way it felt when he was trying to kill us. He would have strangled the breath from me and Vi if he could have."

"Don't speak of that," Victor demanded, shoving Violet's pile of jewelry onto the bedside table. "I prefer to pretend that never happened."

"Bad dreams and not wanting to be alone in the dark is perfectly reasonable when you consider the last few years."

Violet frowned but grinned when she felt the baby kick her hand. "I can't wait to meet Violet Junior. Are you really going to the country?"

"The country air. For Kate and the baby. Whatever it

takes. Bloody hell, Violet, there's another near murder. Kate isn't going anywhere near that. It's dangerous enough for her to be carrying a baby. She's not going anywhere near someone who is poisoning people or whatever they're doing."

"I think he was stabbed. I'm not really sure. I didn't want the details."

"Violet," Victor said very gently. "You know you can't stay here. Jack will be worried."

"I know." Violet turned to look at her twin, and she saw the worry in his gaze. Not only for her, but for Kate. It was nearly debilitating for him, she thought, and she couldn't add to it. "I missed my Vi Junior."

Her lie was ineffective, but he let her get away with it. And because she loved him, she didn't add that she was missing him. He needed to do what he could for Kate, and Vi was only going to help.

"We'll be down soon after you," Vi said idly. "But you should take the auto and motor down. That way Kate can stretch her legs whenever she needs to." Violet followed with a string of orders for Victor to keep Kate comfortable. If he focused on all the little things, he wouldn't obsess over the one he could do nothing about.

Before she left, Violet whispered to Kate about the woman who had defecated on herself to give Kate something stupid to worry over as well.

"Really?" Kate demanded.

"I swear," Violet told her.

Kate's gaze was wide as she slowly said, "Thank you for telling me." Then in a low mutter: "As if swelling up into a walrus and being unable to see my feet wasn't humiliating enough."

CHAPTER TEN

Vi found Jack sitting in the great hall with Hargreaves standing nearby. The two men looked up in utter unsurprise to see Violet heading down the stairs in Victor's robe, wet hair, and no jewelry at all.

"Poor Hargreaves," Violet said as she put her hand on the railing and made her way down the stairs. "You must dream of working for Aunt Agatha."

Hargreaves was not impervious in the slightest when he shook his head. "I consider it both a duty and a privilege to look over you and Mr. Victor, my lady," Hargreaves told her gently.

"Then," Victor said from the head of the stairs, "you'll understand my dismissing you with the understanding that you'll look over Vi."

Hargreaves froze, then relaxed. "Perhaps she needs me a little more than you."

"She showed up here without a coat, an umbrella, or an escort," Victor said to both Jack and Hargreaves.

"I am hardly a child," Violet protested. She thought for a moment and then added, "Though we'd be honored to have you, of course, Hargreaves."

"We'll take your fellow," Victor said. "He'll probably be relieved to have a more standard mistress."

"Out of curiosity," Jack said, as he wrapped his arm around Violet, who was still wearing one of Victor's robes, "what would you have done, Hargreaves? There would have been no stopping Violet when she decided she needed to speak with her brother."

Hargreaves cleared his throat. "Ah, well. I try to think what Mrs. Davies would have told me to do and then I do that."

"And what would have Agatha told you to do?"

"Chase her down with an umbrella and send over dry clothes," Hargreaves answered simply. "Vi wouldn't have been stopped even as a child, you realize."

Jack didn't seem surprised at the answer. He nodded. "I'll speak with Clarkson in the morning. Given his expression when he told me where Vi was, I'm sure he'd prefer working elsewhere."

Hargreaves hesitated and then excused himself.

"Out of curiosity," Victor asked, "did the fellow survive?"

"For now," Jack said. "It's not looking good. The combination of the wound's placement, the fact that he wasn't clean when he was stabbed, and that he was using drugs has put a damper on his ability to survive."

"So the drugs masked the pain of being stabbed?"

"That and the fact that the damage was hidden by his

coat. No one realized he was slowly bleeding out until he couldn't stand anymore. He probably only remained on his feet as long as he did because whatever he used gave him a false sense of strength. When his body processed the drugs, it all caught up with him."

"Somebody tried to kill him, though?" Victor asked. "It wasn't an accident?"

"It's rather hard to make being stabbed in the back an accident. They're trying to find the weapon, but we aren't sure where it happened, and Bobby suggested it was Violet who stabbed him."

"He did what now?" Victor asked.

"He said Violet did it. He said nobody hated him like Violet."

"Is Vi in trouble?" Victor demanded.

"Hardly," Jack said simply. "Of course Violet didn't stab him, and no one believes she did. I even called in Detective Clarkson, who talked to Bobby, laughed when he said Violet stabbed him, and then said he'd find out what he could."

"You called in the fellow who investigated *you*," Victor said, aghast. "What is wrong with you?"

"Ham chose him for me because he's a good detective," Jack said. "Neither of us want Violet wrapped up in another case."

"Why would she be wrapped up in this one?" Victor turned to Violet, wild-eyed. "You can't go sticking your oar in while Jack's working another case and I'm in the country. Denny won't keep an eye on you. By Jove! He'd shove her in if he thought it would be more fun."

"Lila's sister Martha is a suspect. Perhaps even Lila or Denny, though not seriously on either of their cases. I'm sure as soon as Clarkson meets those two, they'll be removed from the suspect list."

"The only thing Denny would murder is a box of chocolates," Victor grumbled. "Why are we associating with such idiots? It's like we're cursed!"

"That's what I said earlier," Violet agreed. "Do we think Martha is innocent?"

"She seemed fairly upset over that whole princess thing."

"Wait, wait, wait," Victor groaned. "It's nearly morning. Go home, go to bed, we'll talk in the morning. I'll bring Kate to keep Violet in check since heaven knows neither of us are any good at it."

Jack didn't argue. He opened the door to Victor's house and took Violet's hand.

"I am," she told him, "perfectly capable of determining if I need a coat or if I should stay out of something, and it is unnecessary to set Hargreaves on me as a personal nanny."

"Victor knows you don't like Cuthbert," Jack said, looking up at the sky. It was too overcast to see anything but shreds of the moon.

"He's like an automaton," Violet agreed.

"Which doesn't bother Victor or Kate but drives you mad."

"It will bug Victor," Violet told Jack smugly. "It'll just take longer and then he'll want Hargreaves back, and we'll say no."

"Instantly and fervently," Jack agreed. He let them into their house and then lifted Violet into his arms and carried her up the stairs.

"I can walk."

"I like holding you."

"Denny wants a baby," Violet told Jack, watching his face for a reaction.

"Denny wants a baby?" Jack laughed. "Can you imagine Denny with a child?"

"Yes," Violet agreed with a laugh of her own. "We'll have to have Hargreaves find him the most tolerant and experienced nanny in all of England."

"Are you saying that because you're ready for a child?"

Violet shook her head as Jack held her with one arm and pushed open the door to their bedroom with the other. "Lila has been asking everyone she knows who has had children about childbirth."

Jack's brows lifted.

"It's terrifying," Violet told Jack.

He set her down in the bath. "I know you want a bath after the evening."

Vi did, so she turned on the water and began haphazardly dumping salts and oils into the filling tub.

"I don't know what to say about the childbirth thing," Jack finally said.

Violet kissed him on the cheek. "You don't have to say anything."

"I don't want you to be afraid either, Vi."

"I want children, Jack. That hasn't changed. I might not be ready yet to have them, but I want them."

Jack shook his head and left the bath, glancing back at her and shaking his head again. Vi laughed, then dropped into the water and scrubbed her body quickly. She had gotten a bit of a chill and even the hot water of the bath didn't solve it fully. She dressed warmly and hurried to bed, crawling in next to Jack and laying her head on his chest as he wrapped one arm around her.

"At least it wasn't someone we love," Violet said, twining their fingers together.

"True." Jack sighed. "Someone must have been shocked that they'd stabbed him and he'd kept moving, even showing up to play at the club. Joshie said Bobby was belligerent when the club opened, shouting at everyone. Was that because he didn't feel well? Or was he stabbed because someone finally had enough?"

"Did the doctor say when he'd been stabbed? Could he narrow it down?"

"No one knows when he took the drugs or how long he'd been bleeding."

Violet pressed her hand against Jack's chest to feel his heartbeat, grateful that his heart wasn't struggling.

"If he hadn't been using those drugs," Violet said, "he might have felt the injury and gotten help in time. What a terrible mess."

"That Heather girl left early. They stayed long enough to check on Bobby, and I got their information. Detective Clarkson will stop by to talk to them."

Violet knew that it meant that Jack had their addresses listed in his notebook.

"What about Sally?"

"She came, she cried over him, answered questions and blamed you too."

"What? What did I do to her?"

"She was dismissed while you were there, Vi."

"Any manager of a business would have dismissed both of them. Bobby, especially, deserved to be let go for how he was behaving. We weren't friends. All of us paid to be there. Any manager would have dismissed an employee for how they were behaving in front of guests. I didn't slap her at her workplace, Bobby did."

Violet sat up, staring down at Jack, who seemed a little amused. She scowled at him, and he wrapped his hand around the back of her neck and pulled just enough to let her know he'd rather she snuggled into his side. Vi flopped back down on his chest, curling into his side and making sure her cold toes were under his leg.

He tugged a strand of hair to let her know he was aware she'd put her cold toes on him on purpose.

"What else did you find out?"

Jack humphed. "No one admitted to stabbing him. They turned on each other, with Martha and Sally yelling at each other and then turning on Heather for realizing that Bobby loved her. Joshie and Henry both seemed shocked, but Joshie made sure that we knew Henry also used drugs and knew where they were coming from. Henry made sure we knew that Bobby owed Joshie rather a lot of money. Both men said the girls were in a constant cat fight over Bobby."

Vi groaned. "Do you think if we were murder suspects we'd all turn on each other?"

"You mean would Lila start telling everyone your secrets and make you look guilty?" Jack laughed. "No, Vi. If any of you were legitimately responsible for a death, it would either be an accident or as close to being deserved as possible. The rest of us would line up and lie without hesitation for each other. They'd never get any of us. Even Rita. She's new, but she's one of us."

"Where did Ham go tonight?" Violet demanded.

Jack grunted and didn't answer.

"What's wrong with him?"

"Vi—"

"Rita is going to Siam. Ham might want to know."

Jack steeled, turning her comfortable pillow to a stone. "*Siam?*"

"That's the plan. By the end of the week. She's says she'll be back for our repeat trip to Cuba or wherever we go after the baby."

"*Siam?*" Jack repeated.

"She agreed to take Martha."

"*Siam!* Has she gone mad?"

"Jack." Violet was gentle as she said, "Those stories about African Safaris and Egypt and India weren't lies."

Slowly Jack relaxed, finally admitting, "I suppose I knew that. I expected her to simply join our trips from now on. Like Lila and Denny do."

"I don't think a hotel by the sea sounds all that intriguing to her." Violet wanted to demand why Ham had left. She wanted to know what was happening with their friends and why Jack wasn't telling her, and she wanted to scold him for keeping secrets all the while knowing she'd have kept Rita's secrets if she were asked.

Was there something Violet could do to help Ham and Rita see that they'd fallen in love or was it better to stay out of it? Maybe the best thing was to focus on the problem ahead of her and simply love and support Rita and Ham as best she could.

CHAPTER ELEVEN

*V*iolet woke screaming from the nightmare of someone stabbing Victor and Kate's baby. Jack placed his hand on her stomach and whispered, "It's all right, love. It's all right."

"It's not," Violet gasped, her heart racing so much it hurt. "It's not. It was the baby. She needed me, and I couldn't get her, and then they took her away from me."

"The baby is safe, Vi. I promise, she's safe."

"She wasn't though," Violet said, turning into Jack's side. "She wasn't."

Jack didn't argue with her any further. He rubbed her back until she fell back asleep.

The sun was well and truly up when she woke. She felt as though someone had beat her and her head ached. She'd had several cocktails, but she knew the headache was from the dreams rather than the drinks. Violet slowly rose, ringing the bell. Usually she dressed herself and then appeared for breakfast, but today was a day where Violet was going to have coffee delivered to her room and sip it in the bath with two aspirin until she felt slightly human.

Beatrice appeared in Violet's room and Violet said, "You're a secretary now, my love."

"Mr. Wakefield asked me to look after you today."

"Did he leave already?"

"Just after dawn, my lady. He switched Mr. Cuthbert with Mr. Hargreaves?"

Violet nodded. "Victor dismissed Hargreaves with the understanding he'd look after me. I, apparently, need babysitting."

Beatrice grinned. "I'm glad that he'll be here. Mr. Cuthbert is very professional," she added rather diplomatically.

"He's a very effective automaton," Violet agreed and Beatrice laughed. "I need coffee and aspirin, darling."

Violet dropped into the bath with her eye mask replaced on her face. She slowly pushed it back when the door to her bath opened and found Beatrice with the coffee. Violet took it and sipped slowly until the headache moved from a constant, throbbing ache to a dull steady pain. After she'd soaked until the water turned tepid, she returned to her bedroom wrapped in one of her kimonos and found that Beatrice had arrived with the dogs.

"Did you name the puppy?" Beatrice asked as Vi lifted the little fellow up.

"Holmes," Vi replied, accepting his kisses. "Did everyone stay?"

"No one else has come down from their rooms except for Mr. Denny, who arranged for the chalkboards from Mr. Victor's house to arrive. Mr. Victor sent over Hargreaves and a request to send for them when you appear for breakfast."

Violet nodded, holding back a sigh. "Give me a dress, darling. Anything."

Beatrice pulled out a cream dress with an overlay of lace and beading along the hem and short sleeves. Violet put it on without comment, adding the pink pearl earbobs Jack had bought in Madrid. She dressed slowly and acknowledged to herself that Denny would never let her get away without at least discussing what had happened to Bobby.

Violet made her way down to the breakfast room and found Hargreaves standing at the door. "How are you today, Hargreaves?"

"Quite well, my lady," he said.

Violet reached out and squeezed his hand. It was surprising how much his presence made her house truly feel like home. He followed her into the room and watched as she made herself another cup of coffee. There might not be enough, she thought, to get through the day. "Thank you for coming."

"I am happy to look after either of you, my lady."

"I'm afraid we're so entwined that looking after one of us is looking after the other. Mr. Cuthbert will work better with Kate, I think."

When Violet sat down only with the coffee, Mr. Hargreaves crossed to the buffet and made her a plate with toast and fruit. Violet laughed when he placed it in front of her. "Jack?"

"Yes, my lady," Hargreaves said just as Denny entered the room.

"The chalkboards have arrived," Denny said, happily

rubbing his hands together. "I heard you had bad dreams. Darling Vi, don't be sad. This will be fun. At least it isn't someone we liked."

"Is he dead?" Violet gasped.

Denny paused and then nodded slowly. "He didn't make it through the night. Detective Clarkson appeared at the door and then lingered about while Jack went to talk to Victor. Vi, you matter more to Jack than the case." He said it with as much soberness as Denny ever got, and, as usual, it didn't last as he continued gleefully. "He had me on the suspect list. I added my name to the board as the first suspect but Clarkson told me if I were the one who stabbed the bloke, he would give up detecting and take up being a fishmonger."

Violet watched Denny build a hefty plate.

"Where is Lila?"

"She's fooling around with her makeup."

Violet considered the toast and fruit in front of her and then popped a strawberry into her mouth. It didn't make her stomach roll, so she ate another and then tried the toast. Her stomach didn't rebel again, so Violet finished the toast. She wondered if that was how Kate had spent the past several months eating, testing each bite.

Rita arrived just as Violet was standing to leave for the parlor. "I just want tea. I'll follow you in a moment."

Lila was already in the parlor when they arrived, and Kate and Victor had arrived as well. To Violet's surprise, Detective Clarkson and Jack were also there.

Violet lifted a brow and Jack shrugged, but Detective Clarkson was in a full flush. "It's become something of a legend at Scotland Yard that your method works."

"You mean writing names on the chalkboard and gossiping?"

Detective Clarkson paused, but then he gave her a nod. "Jack and I agree that we'd like this case to be over quickly and ensure both your safety and the safety of everyone involved."

Violet crossed to the board since she wasn't going to get out of it. Denny had already listed all the names. They read:

DENNY LANCASTER — Denny doesn't care if Bobby is a criminal. To be perfectly transparent, Denny thinks Bobby is a wart who deserved to be stabbed.

LILA LANCASTER— Lila wouldn't stab anyone just because the blood might ruin her dress or her shoes.

VIOLET WAKEFIELD—Violet would stab someone without question. She's an ominous woman who will protect those she loves. She does not, however, love Bobby. Unless she fell in love with him in an instant and has already cuckolded poor Jack.

MARTHA POTTER (PRINCESS)—Princess has always been trouble. She once broke a poor innocent doll in a rage. If she would do that as a child, what would she do when she was snubbed by a low-class criminal who manipulated her pin money out of her?

HEATHER FLYE—She snores excellently and apparently can pull a rescue out of a by-passer—like Vi—without even fluttering her lashes or releasing a manipulative tear.

SALLY—Terrible dancer, terrible dance instructor. Completely untrustworthy.

JOSHIE—The man can play trumpet with soul and heart and could not possibly have stabbed anyone and then played so perfectly after. Certainly innocent.

THAT OTHER GUY—does anyone remember his name? The bass guy. Probably a criminal. Who knows?

Violet shook her head at the chalkboard. "You've been busy this morning."

"It's why I was so hungry. Brainwork will wear you out. Make you need to recover. A nap is likely."

"Don't you nap daily?" Violet asked Denny, who grinned.

"It'll never be so well-earned."

"Are they always like this?" Detective Clarkson asked.

"Yes," Jack said evenly and then rose to refill his coffee.

Violet erased the board. "Ring for Beatrice, would you?" she asked Victor.

As he did so, Violet rewrote the names in the same order.

DENNY LANCASTER

LILA LANCASTER

VIOLET WAKEFIELD

She paused at her own name with her new last name, feeling a surreal rush of happiness. Considering the terror that had woken her in the night, the happiness surprised her, but she attributed it to the knowledge that the people she loved most in the world were safe and sitting in her new parlor.

MARTHA POTTER—

"Add princess," Denny said. "She'll love that when we demand explanations."

Vi added princess. It was then that she paused and considered the rest of the names. The most likely people to have stabbed Bobby were those who were closest to him. At least in normal circumstances. But this was a bloke who ran underground dance clubs in abandoned buildings. Surely his business itself could have been the reason for the murder.

"What about business partners?" Vi asked.

"Leave those to Clarkson and the Yard," Jack answered. She smiled at him, a bit relieved to keep their involvement to a minimum.

"Really," she said, agreeing, "we just need to clear Martha so she can go to Siam with Rita."

"You aren't going to Siam, are you, Rita?" Jack asked.

"Oh, I'm going," Rita replied. "I hear their oceans are lovely."

"It can't be safe," Clarkson said, his mouth open with shock.

"I believe a man we associated with was stabbed just the other night in London and none of us even realized he was bleeding," she told him wryly. "At least in Siam, I know I need to be on my guard and careful."

Detective Clarkson stared at Jack. "Your friends are odd." No one argued with him.

Violet wrote down the names of every one of her friends who had been present when Bobby could have been stabbed and then included all of the associates of his that they'd met. When she was finished, it read:

DENNY LANCASTER
LILA LANCASTER
VIOLET WAKEFIELD
MARTHA POTTER- PRINCESS
JACK WAKEFIELD
RITA RUSSELL
HEATHER FLYE
SALLY
JOSHIE
HENRY

DOOR MAN

Violet stared at the list and then she wrote a series of questions on the second chalkboard.

BOBBY — Who wanted to kill Bobby? Who had a reason? Did Martha stab him because she realized he was pursuing her for the money? Did Joshie kill him because Bobby owed him money? Did Henry kill him because Bobby was a jerk who was manipulating the girls? Did Sally kill him because he was violent with her and got her dismissed from her job at the tango club?

Did all the girls really prefer Bobby over Joshie and Henry? Perhaps there were passing lovers that created a quiet hatred? What was so special about him over the more-talented Joshie or the kinder Henry?

Violet turned back to the first chalkboard and started on her own name as Detective Clarkson asked, "Is this how it usually goes?"

Jack added some whiskey to his coffee and then poured some into Clarkson's.

"I'm working," he protested.

"You're going to need it. So far you've seen Denny and Lila on good behavior."

Clarkson stared for a moment and then shrugged and sipped his tea.

"I could just make cocktails," Victor offered.

"It isn't even time for afternoon tea," Clarkson said, shocked.

"We don't really obey the clock," Victor told Clarkson.

"We're far too spoiled to be dictated to by clocks," Lila said lazily. "Dear Victor, I do think your wife needs something to put those ham hocks she calls ankles on."

"You are mean," Kate told Lila. "Wait until it's you."

"Don't say such things." Lila shuddered, and then made Kate a cup of tea.

"This doesn't make calling my feet ham hocks better," Kate said as she accepted the tea.

Violet ignored them both and cocked her head at the chalkboard.

VIOLET WAKEFIELD— Victim claimed she stabbed him. Violet spent the entirety of the evening with Jack, Lila, Martha, and Rita. There was no opportunity to have stabbed Bobby without a witness. Why did he claim it had been Violet who tried to kill him?

Violet sniffed as she paced in front of her question. Whoever stabbed Bobby had a motive. Was he simply confused by the drugs and the blood loss? Perhaps he remembered that he was angry with Violet over the situation with Heather. If so, he might have conflated his anger with who hurt him. But what if he wasn't confused? What if he realized who had stabbed him?

She added a line to the section under her name: If he knew who killed him and claimed it was Violet, he must have loved the killer enough to lie with his dying breath.

CHAPTER TWELVE

"*A*h," Clarkson said, reading the board as Violet played with her wedding ring, pacing.

"Don't interrupt," Denny said. "The way her mind works is my favorite part. Except for when she corners someone and makes them confess."

Violet shot Denny a quelling look. It wasn't as though she were putting on a show. She wrote under Jack's name next.

JACK WAKEFIELD — No motive. No opportunity to stab Bobby. Even if Jack hated Bobby, why would Jack stab Bobby when connections at Scotland Yard could destroy him easily?

"Perhaps," Detective Clarkson said, "because Bobby threatened you. I understand that he did."

Violet shrugged, unbothered by Clarkson's assertion. Jack hadn't had a chance to stab Bobby and Clarkson wouldn't be able to get around that.

"You know," Lila added idly, "if Jack were going to murder

anyone, it would be someone who threatened Vi, *and* if Bobby wanted revenge for his death, he'd try to pin his murder on Vi. Nothing would torture either of them more than being separated."

"Lila, darling," Victor said, "shut your impish mouth."

Violet glanced over to wink at her brother and then went to Lila's name. Vi wrote:

Too lazy to murder.

Under Denny, Violet wrote:

Even lazier.

Violet studied the board before glancing at her friends, thinking. No one spoke as she returned to the board.

RITA RUSSELL. No fan of Bobby, but no chance to kill him either. She arrived late to the tango club and then spent the rest of the evening in direct contact with her friends.

"Is she putting all of your names on there just to satisfy me?" Clarkson asked Jack as though the rest of them weren't present.

"Maybe," Jack replied. "Sometimes she does it just for fun. Sometimes she does it because she knows they're a real suspect even if she doesn't believe one of us killed whoever died."

Violet glanced at both of them. "I am not a performing monkey. I'd like to see Martha on her way before her father arrives and that is all that is happening here. Bobby was a nasty wart and probably deserved to be stabbed even if I disagree with murder itself."

"That makes no sense," Clarkson told Violet.

She shrugged in reply.

Victor glanced over her board. "The key is the claim that Violet was the killer," he announced, but he was speaking to

Vi. He crossed to his twin and stood next to her, holding his hand out for the chalk. She handed it over and he crossed through all of their friends' names, leaving only the people they'd met who had associated with Bobby and worked with him.

"If he wasn't confused," Victor said, "then he was protecting one of these people. It rules out all of his business contacts as well. If this were one of our books—I'd focus on these." Victor circled the names:

Martha, Sally, and Heather.

"I agree," Violet said.

"I don't," Lila objected. "If it is Martha, my mother will claim it's my fault from now until the end of time. We will meet at the pearly gates of heaven and Mother will remind me of how she trusted me with Martha and I failed."

Violet drew a line under Heather's name. "Bobby actually said he loved her. She showed up at the warehouse after she had gone home. Maybe she realized that he had lied to her about her parents?"

Rita leaned forward. "You know, we don't know why Heather didn't go home before. It took her being defenseless and drugged to want to go home. Perhaps the reason she didn't go was because of something Bobby had said to her. Maybe he had even lied to her. What if she'd wanted to go home for some time, and he'd convinced her—through lies— that her parents wouldn't take her back?"

Kate sniffed and Violet glanced back to see her rubbing her baby. "It won't happen to Violet Junior," Violet told her sister-in-law as though Violet herself hadn't woken terrified for the baby in the middle of the night.

"What a world we live in," Kate said, and a tear rolled

down her face. Victor started towards her, and she ordered, "Leave it be. It's just…" But she couldn't finish.

"Anna George told me she'd never cried so much as she did when she was expecting," Lila said, watching Kate as though she were mysterious. "Said she cried every single day from before she realized she was with child all the way through to when her baby turned half a year old."

Victor cleared his throat, and Violet elbowed him when she realized he'd paled.

"What's a few tears?" Denny asked Lila. "We'll buy a stockpile of handkerchiefs. We're going to be the most amazing parents."

Violet turned back to the chalkboard. "We need to know how much money Bobby owed Joshie and whether it was enough for Joshie to risk his freedom over."

Jack crossed his legs. "You can't simply ask him that and expect him to answer honestly, Vi. He'd lie if he killed Bobby *or* if he realizes it is enough money to implicate him."

"He's probably already returned to his barrister father," Violet added. "If there's anything to get one to mend the bridges between father and son, it'll be the threat of prison. We need Martha."

"She's a suspect," Clarkson protested.

"But she didn't do it," Violet told him.

"How do you know?"

"Because," Violet told him, "she'd already made other plans. Princess is the right term for her. She romanticized these people, realized they were mocking her, and decided to put her crown back on."

"That makes no sense," Clarkson said.

"Whoever stabbed him didn't do it in a calculated

maneuver. They flew into a rage. Martha might have killed him when she heard him refer to her as princess, but we were all there. She did talk to Sally for a bit without us present, but she came back resolved to leave England and travel with Rita."

"That doesn't mean she didn't stab him," Clarkson protested. "It proves nothing."

"They don't care about that," Jack told Clarkson and watched him groan.

"How do they find murderers?"

"It's that whole plot bit," Jack said dryly. "They try to find the details of the story and add things up."

"There's no proof that way."

"They aren't detectives," Jack told Clarkson. "They don't care about fingerprints and what not. They care about gossip and motives and whether they'd believe it. None of them can see Martha as the murderer, so they don't take her seriously."

Clarkson groaned again and then shook his head. "I can't waste my time this way. What a bunch of nonsense. I can only assume that they've stumbled across the killer by sheer happenstance in the past. Bloody hell, Jack, you're a well-respected detective. I don't know how you can sit there and listen to this."

"I suppose," Jack said easily, "Vi and her friends just aren't to your taste."

"I don't see how they are to yours," Clarkson said. "Let alone Barnes."

"By their fruits, ye shall know them," Rita told Clarkson cheekily and then grinned as he flushed and left.

"By Jove!" Denny declared. "That took forever. I thought he'd never go once Jack started pouring whiskey and

Clarkson didn't stalk out offended. He was ruining all my fun with that gaze weighing our actions and finding us wanting."

Lila laughed. "His exit requires a chocolate cocktail, I think."

Victor moved to the bar while Rita demanded, "Is that what you did when I first started coming by?"

"I don't think so," Lila said. "We mostly liked you from the beginning."

"Any girl who'd been on a safari," Denny added, "is our kind of people. Then there's how Ham stares at you. That's particularly entertaining. I'm not ready for him to stop."

"Denny!" Lila hissed.

"Oh," Denny said, not sounding repentant. "Was I not supposed to talk about that?"

Lila huffed and then told Victor, "You had better go heavy on Rita's cocktails. Denny is considering playing matchmaker."

"It just makes sense," Denny added. "Otherwise they'll eventually marry someone else, and we'll have to add two more to our group. No one wants our little family to become overcrowded. We haven't even started adding the little mites yet."

Rita's blond complexion and blue eyes truly gave her the ability to turn a brilliant red, Violet thought as she crossed to Denny. "Leave it," she warned him, "or you can't have any more cocktails."

Denny gasped. "Violet, that's just cruel."

"So is teasing Rita about Ham."

"But Ham loves her. Probably. Maybe. Ham certainly thinks she's quite pretty."

Violet kicked Denny in the shin and told him precisely,

"Anyone with eyes thinks Rita is pretty. She's quite lovely, as I'm sure you've noticed."

"I haven't," Denny lied. "I only have eyes for my wife."

"Liars go to hell," Violet told him. "That's one of the Ten Commandments."

"You lie all the time."

Violet winked at him. "At least we'll have each other in our fiery pit."

"Too true," Denny said, lifting his teacup in salute. "To our eternity burning, dear one."

"Shall we get back to work?" Jack took the tray of cocktails and passed them around. "Also, Violet will be spending her eternity with me even if I have to drag her out of hell."

"I don't think that's how hell works," Denny told Jack seriously. "If anyone would escape hell, it would be those sent there. If you could just get out, it wouldn't be much of a punishment, would it?"

"Oh my goodness," Rita moaned. "Would you please return your attention to clearing your sister-in-law?"

"I'm not all that concerned," Denny whispered loudly to Rita. "I didn't like Martha as a child. Let alone now."

"Denny," Lila said, "we need to clear her name and get rid of her. If you keep making her sound bad, we won't be able to foist her off on Rita."

Rita sighed and threw herself back on the sofa while Violet crossed to the bell and rang for Beatrice. She needed Martha and the details of Bobby's life that only a girl half-in-love and trying him on for size in her imagination would discover.

CHAPTER THIRTEEN

*V*iolet sighed and threw herself on the Chesterfield. "My head hurts."

Jack pulled her up and sat down underneath her. "You'll feel better if you could sleep better."

"Is she having nightmares again?"

"Yes," Jack said, sounding as frustrated as Violet felt, "about—"

Violet smacked him. "People being stabbed."

"People?" Victor asked suspiciously.

"People," Violet lied.

"Lie," Victor declared, and Violet straightened enough to give him a commanding look until he held up his hands in surrender.

"Let's get back to work while we wait for your idiot sister," Violet said, standing quickly to exorcise the memories of the baby being stabbed from a hand in the dark. Jack's arms tightened around her as she rose, but he released her.

The chalkboard of her notes so far read:

LILA LANCASTER— Too lazy to murder.

DENNY LANCASTER— Even lazier.

VIOLET WAKEFIELD— Victim claimed she stabbed him. Violet spent the entirety of the evening with Jack, Lila, Martha, and Rita. There was no opportunity to have stabbed Bobby without a witness. Why did he claim it had been Violet who tried to kill him? If he knew who killed him and claimed it was Violet, he must have loved them enough to lie with his dying breath.

MARTHA POTTER—PRINCESS.

JACK WAKEFIELD — No motive. No opportunity to stab Bobby. Even if Jack hated Bobby, why would Jack stab Bobby when connections at Scotland Yard could destroy him easily?

RITA RUSSELL —No fan of Bobby, but no chance to kill him either. She arrived late to the tango club and then spent the rest of the evening in direct contact with her friends.

HEATHER FLYE-

SALLY —

JOSHIE—

HENRY —

DOOR MAN —

Violet started with Martha since experience had taught her that seeing your own name on the suspect list made people far more likely to be open. She wrote after Martha's name:

The slumming princess has a large motive for having

killed Bobby. He had led her to believe that his criminal activities was somehow more righteous than being born wealthy—as though "grit" and "sweat" in committing crimes was to be respected. Did Martha help in the selling of drugs? Did Martha help find the venues and the rich marks like Denny and Violet to scam out of their money?

Violet stepped back to read what she'd written and then glanced back and winked at Lila as Vi added:

Surely Mr. Potter will lock down Martha's inheritance if he realizes how she's been spending her time. Any freedom she has will be whisked away, and she'll either have to truly work to support herself or obey the dictates of her uptight family.

Denny giggled at that as Violet waxed almost poetic in adding:

No more parties. No more modern dresses. Married off to the first righteous man who comes along unless she risks everything like Lila did, marrying for love and knowing her family might disown her.

Violet stepped back.

"Too much more and you'll clue her in," Lila warned. "She isn't entirely stupid. Put some stuff on the board about the others. Something about how Bobby loved Heather the most and Martha and Sally were just easy marks."

"You're cruel, wife," Denny told Lila.

"You like it," Rita said.

"I do," Denny agreed, blowing Lila a kiss.

Violet wrote:

HEATHER — Bobby's true love.

SALLY — Bobby's long-time friend and companion. Perhaps his closest friend. The keeper of his secrets. The person who knew him the best.

"You are diabolical, Vi," Jack said. "If someone wrote any of that about you, I'd be tempted to track them down and throw them on a ship to China."

"You'd have to believe it, first."

"And she does have one such person in her life." Victor clapped Jack on his back.

Jack shook his head at Victor and said, "Martha might not know what we need to know, and she'll be more likely to talk if I'm not here. I'm going to speak to the doctor and see if he can give me a time frame on when Bobby might have been stabbed. We'd rule out Heather, at the least, if we knew it happened at the tango club, and Martha if we knew it happened after."

Violet kissed Jack's cheek as he left and then turned back to the board, filling in the information for Joshie.

JOSHIE— Was owed money by Bobby. Enough to kill over?

HENRY— Drug-user with Bobby. Did they sell the drugs at these parties together? Perhaps there was a scuffle over being declined drugs. Perhaps Henry owed Bobby money for drugs and was turned down when he wanted more.

"People do get squirrelly over drugs," Victor said. "My goodness, how much time has passed since breakfast and what do I have to do for a cucumber sandwich?"

He glanced at Kate and noticed she'd fallen asleep while they'd been talking.

"Poor love," Victor said. "I think we're never having another baby."

"I don't think you can make that decision, old man," Denny said. "You have to leave it to Kate."

"Says the man harassing his wife for a baby."

"They're not all as bad as Kate. My cousin glowed the whole time. She was never prettier than when she was expecting."

Violet rolled her eyes, and Rita said, "Women have been having children for ages. There was a woman in India who was sick the whole of her first child. The second child, she never seemed healthier."

"I don't think any of us are in a position to discuss it," Violet said. "Kate will do what she wants and Victor will want what she wants. What happens with you two," Violet told Lila and Denny, "is none of the rest of our business."

"But if we name the baby Vi," Denny asked, "you'll leave her some money too, right? Because I expect Lila and I will spend all we have."

Violet sighed, knowing it was most likely. "I could help with that."

"I'm taking Kate home," Victor announced and then lifted her into his arms. Surely he realized that she was going to wake the second the outside air hit her even if she didn't wake before they left the house.

The others said their quiet goodbyes.

"I was hoping you would," Denny said, continuing the conversation. "See Lila, I told you Violet would do it for us."

Violet scowled at Denny, but he just giggled as he usually did. Violet would happily have helped him, but that didn't mean she didn't want to smack him a little. "Why do I like you?"

"I'm like a fungus. You just can't get rid of me."

"Oh, laddie," Lila said. "You really are contagious."

Violet shook her head, but it raised another thought. "I need to have my stepmother over before we leave."

"May I be there?" Denny demanded.

"No," Lila told him, "but I'll be."

"But I want to," Denny whined.

Violet ignored both of them. She paced the room. "Have you noticed that our lives have gotten complicated? Children, murders, re-doing houses, placating stepmothers, seeing your children don't starve?"

"My life feels the same," Rita said with a smirk. She winked at Violet's frustrated glance. "It's not my fault you got married and bought a house instead of moving into a hotel. I suppose your stepmother isn't your fault, but the rest—"

"Careful, miss," Violet told Rita. "Your father re-married once. He might again."

"He had two murdered wives," Rita said. "I think he feels cursed."

"He's still a handsome man," Lila said to Denny's groan.

"And rich," Violet added when she noticed that Martha had arrived with Hargreaves and Beatrice. "Very rich."

"Who is rich and handsome?" Martha asked.

Rita's gaze widened and she shot Violet a vengeful glance, but it was ruined at the sound of Denny's hysterical giggles.

"I'll have the tea tray in soon, my lady," Hargreaves said. He glanced the room over and then nodded to Beatrice, who cleared the scattering of teacups and cocktails glasses onto a tray. Hargreaves held the door open for her.

Violet's head cocked as she examined Martha. The girl was lushly beautiful, Violet had to admit. For men who preferred a curvaceous woman, Martha—like Lila—was a perfect example.

"Who is rich and handsome?" Martha asked.

"Rita's father," Violet said. "You know he's already married young and beautiful once."

"What happened to her?" Martha demanded, her gaze flicking from Rita to Denny to Violet.

"She was murdered horribly," Rita told Martha. "My father was a suspect."

Denny's giggles turned into a hysterical howl. "Too late," Denny said, wiping tears, "the magic words of handsome and rich have been said."

Violet shot Rita a telling glance before speaking to Martha. "You can keep pursuing the authentic grit and sweat and potential criminals, or we could introduce you to rich and handsome men. We know many."

Martha's gaze narrowed, finally looking around. "What do you want?"

"Just the truth," Violet told her. "We need the details to clear you. Surely you know as the spurned upper class lover of a criminal, who was being led on while he pursued his true love, you are who Scotland Yard is considering for the most likely killer. They think you just grabbed a knife and stabbed him and then stayed with us when you saw him walking around. It must have been like seeing the walking dead. Wasn't it?"

Martha's gaze moved between then, wide and scared. "But, that's not true. I didn't stab him. I would never have."

"Never cross a woman scorned," Violet reminded her. "Men have been writing plays and books about the danger of a spurned, abandoned lover for generations. Scotland Yard can't imagine anything else."

"Jack doesn't think that, does he? He doesn't. He was nice to me when I cried over Bobby."

Violet's gaze narrowed on Martha, and she heard Denny's, "Oh-ho," but Violet didn't react.

"It isn't Jack's case," Violet told Martha flatly. "Jack doesn't get to vote. Why are you protecting them anyway? I'd think you'd want to help find whoever killed the man you thought you loved."

Martha scowled. "I never loved him. I just loved watching Lila squirm. He was fun."

"That feels like an edited version of events," Denny announced. "She's changing her tune now that she knows they called her princess and laughed about taking her money."

"You don't know that they laughed at me."

"We did," Denny told Martha.

"Be quiet," Violet told Denny. "No one laughed at you. We girls knows what it's like to fall for a man who doesn't treat you right."

"Lila doesn't."

"Lila saw me suffer," Violet lied. "We've known Rita long enough to see her suffer as well."

"Hear, hear," Rita said, and Violet glanced over, hearing too much truth in that statement. What *had* Ham done to Rita and why was she so determined to go to Siam?

"The men don't understand," Violet told Martha. "We risk so much more than they do. We don't have the same rights. The same protections aren't in place for us."

Martha's lip quivered. "It's not fair."

"I know," Violet said so very gently, "I know."

"I only want someone who loves me like Jack loves you, like Denny loves Lila."

CHAPTER FOURTEEN

"*L*ike Bobby loved Heather?" Violet asked in that same gentle voice.

Martha scoffed and shook her head. "It's like you said, Vi. Heather didn't even use drugs on her own. Bobby would slip them into her drink or push her into using them. He didn't like it when she didn't use them because Heather didn't like how he acted when he was on drugs. His solution was to slip some to her. He didn't do it so often that she needed them like he did. She would never trust him after, you know. They'd get out of her system, and it would take him weeks to catch her unaware again."

Violet would have made notes, but she didn't want to stop the flow of Martha's story.

"My goodness, Martha, why did you find him attractive?" Lila didn't sound lazy—she sound disgusted, but Martha didn't seem to notice, thank goodness.

Rita placed a hand on Lila to quiet her as Violet said, "It's funny what women will do if they're in love."

"He was compelling when he wanted to be," Martha said. She scowled and then admitted, "Usually when he wanted money for something. He always made it seem like he was doing me a favor taking money off of my hands."

Martha glanced over her shoulder, but her gaze didn't land on Denny or Lila, which was good because the disgust on their faces might have convinced her to stay silent.

"What about Sally?" Vi asked, drawing her attention again.

Martha shook her head. "I—" Violet lifted a brow when she stopped, so Martha continued. "It was obvious that she loved him. I just thought, well, he doesn't love her. Why is she hanging about, hoping? Time for her to find someone else, but she wouldn't. She ran around, waiting for him to look her way."

Violet wanted to scream at Martha, Why did you like him? Why would you like anyone who treated someone that way? Vi wanted to take Heather and shake her. Why had she gone back to that fiend time and again? And Sally, it seemed like he treated her like a servant. Why would any girl put up with that nonsense?

"What about Henry?" she asked instead. "Did they argue?"

Martha shook her head. "Not really."

"Henry uses drugs too, right?"

Martha paused and then nodded. Denny mumbled something to Lila, but again, Martha was so concerned with her own story and the comments on the chalkboard about her that she didn't seem to be aware that Denny and Lila were horrified.

"Henry comes to Bobby, gets his drugs, and works. He has another job, during the day, that sees to his rooms and food and such. He wasn't as...sucked in as Bobby. Bobby got mean when he didn't have drugs. Henry just found a way to get what he wanted. He's careful too. As careful as you can be."

Violet didn't scoff, but Rita and Denny were choking back their replies to that idea.

"What about Joshie?"

"Joshie just wants to play music," Martha said. "He doesn't see anything but the music. Except Heather sometimes, but not because he cares for her. He introduced her to Bobby. They needed a pianist, and then they brought her in. I think he felt bad about introducing her to Bobby. You'd see Joshie talking to her on the side. Trying to persuade her to leave the life behind. To go home."

Hargreaves appeared with the loaded tea trays and the fresh coffee and tea. Violet's headache had returned, and she begged a few aspirin and found her request echoed by Lila and Denny as well. Both of them were staring at Martha as though she'd grown an extra head, and Violet didn't blame them in the least. As far as she was concerned, Lila's little sister was one of the biggest fools Violet had ever met.

"How do we get the rest of them to talk?" Violet asked.

Martha took the cup of tea that Violet made her. Vi returned to pour herself a full cup of Turkish coffee.

"There are cucumber sandwiches," Hargreaves told Violet with an emphasized expression.

She nodded and took one. It would have to be enough.

Her headache had returned in full force and the aspirin and coffee were making her stomach hurt as well. Perhaps she'd feel better if she ate something else, but she didn't think anything but a nap would solve it all.

"Martha," Vi asked, "do you think you could get Heather to come here?"

Martha shook her head.

"Don't forget that you're the suspect," Lila told her sister. "Don't forget Father is coming, and if he realizes, he won't let you gallivant about with Rita."

"I need a change of scenery."

"You won't get a bigger one than Siam," Rita told Martha. "If you're sure you want to come."

"Anywhere but here."

"I certainly understand that sentiment," Rita said, "but I won't help you flee Scotland Yard."

"May I tell her that she's the main suspect?" Martha asked suddenly. "If we were to lie to her, she might talk then."

Violet's gaze darted to Denny, who was grinning. He was the one who answered. "That *might* work. Making someone believe they're in trouble is a…ah, it's a cruel machination."

"Better her than me," Martha snapped.

"Indeed," Denny choked out and then shoved a sandwich into his mouth before Martha realized he was fighting back a laugh.

"Do take smaller bites, Denny." Martha shook her head. "You're not an animal or a child."

Lila, Rita, and Violet carefully avoided looking at each other.

"Bring her by in the morning," Violet told Martha, "if you

can. Tell her that I know a private investigator who can help her."

"Do bring in the pretty one," Rita said. "He adds so much to the scenery."

"I agree with that sentiment." Violet grinned.

She nodded and rang the bell for Hargreaves. They'd need him to send for the private investigator they'd employed to help clear Jack's name. The man would do anything for his client, and Violet wasn't above having him help her manipulate the players in this case to find the truth.

"Martha is stupid to a level that is shocking," Violet told Jack that night.

"So you had to hire the angel-devil detective. He's a step above a criminal, Violet."

"These aren't our people, Jack," Violet said. "They aren't going to tell us their secrets. We can't believe that Henry is a good guy who controls his drug use because Martha says so. We can't trust that Joshie isn't in love with Heather because Martha says it was brotherly. We need someone who will discover their secrets for us. Someone who doesn't care what they are but will chase them to the ground."

"Why do you have to be involved at all?"

"Martha is too stupid to live. Someone has to help her. There is no way she isn't on Detective Clarkson's list of suspects and probably at the top."

Jack rubbed his jaw, examining the stubble in the mirror before turning to Violet. He shook his head. "I suppose I fell in love with you because you looked after the defenseless. It's an appealing trait in a person who should be even more spoilt and stupid than Martha."

Violet sat down on his lap, wrapping her arms around his neck. "I fell in love with you because you didn't see me as another spoilt, stupid lady. I guess we really are a match made in heaven."

Jack laughed against her lips, kissed her, and then leaned back. "Ask."

"Who does Clarkson prefer for the crime?"

Jack frowned as he admitted, "Martha. The doctor won't say when he thought Bobby was stabbed, so it could be Martha when she disappeared at the tango club. The only ones who it couldn't be is you and Rita."

Violet pressed her forehead against Jack's chest, listening to his heartbeat, and knew she was a maudlin fool when the sound of it gave her peace. "Who do you think did it?"

"There's no evidence trapping anyone right now. Clarkson's men need to find the weapon, if they can."

"You still have a theory."

"I lean towards Joshie or Heather. Sally took Bobby's neglect and abuse for too long to think she'd turn on him after all that time. Joshie could easily have feelings for Heather. He had to have guessed she went home, and unlike Bobby, Joshie wouldn't be someone her parents would hate."

Violet considered. "I don't think we should discount Sally, but I'd like to think it was Heather standing up for herself after all his abuse. Really, however, I'd prefer it was that fellow at the door. You know what pauses me?"

Jack tilted his head for the answer, but didn't wait for it. Instead he peppered her face with light, soft kisses. Violet was distracted until he asked, "What pauses you, love?"

"Someone stabbed Bobby and he didn't react. He didn't stagger and call for help. He didn't try to get revenge. He didn't fall down dead. Whoever stabbed him—it was in the back—it must have been this act of rage, but then he just kept walking around. One of them knew he'd been stabbed. They must have been going mad wondering what was happening."

Jack rubbed his chin along his jaw. "So who is the best actress of them all?"

"Not Martha," Violet told him and Jack nodded.

"Not Martha." He sighed. "It never ceases to amaze me what people do to each other. You would think that whoever stabbed him would have run. Tried to hide or get away or finish the job even, but to just casually wait? That takes a coldness that I wish I had a harder time imagining."

"It seems all too possible after the cases I've seen," Violet told him. "It must be infinitely worse for you with all that you've seen."

"Before you, Vi, it was slowly ruining me."

Jack lifted Violet from the chair and carried her to the bed. He laid her down and then stretched out next to her, pressing another kiss to her forehead and then running more along her jaw. In the moments before they slept, he showed her once again what it was to be cherished and adored.

CHAPTER FIFTEEN

*I*t took Martha three days to get Heather to Violet's house. During that time, they'd discovered that Bobby had owed a lot of money to a lot of people. They were, however, all rather like Martha and Joshie. Fools with too much money who'd come into his web.

"It seems to me," Rita said, "that whoever killed him was someone who knew him well enough to see through his lies."

"I'd like to know why Clarkson's men haven't found the weapon yet," Jack said. "Someone might have snapped and killed Bobby, but they aren't evil geniuses. Finding the weapon could break the whole case open and draw it to a conclusion."

Their conversation fell to an immediate stop when Heather was presented at the door with her mother. Violet lifted a brow at Martha, but she shrugged. Heather and her mother walked into the room and took the seat that was offered along with the cup of tea. Heather didn't drink the tea and Violet watched her fiddle with the cup for a long while.

Heather's mother finally spoke. "I understand I have you to thank for returning my daughter to me, Lady Violet."

"Just Vi, please," Violet said, hoping it would set the woman at ease, but if anything she stiffened.

"I'm sorry, Lady Violet," Mrs. Flye said. "My daughter and I have heard of your reputation."

"I must seem like a monster to you then," Violet said. "An interfering spoiled woman who wiles away an afternoon digging through people's secrets."

"Perhaps," Mrs. Flye said stiffly.

"Of course," Violet said easily, "if I didn't interfere and meddle, I'd have left your daughter in the state I found her."

Mrs. Flye's gaze darted to Violet, and the woman's mouth pursed. Her gaze moved to her daughter and she stiffened.

"I am not a monster," Violet told Mrs. Flye. "I have no desire to see your daughter suffer or be accused of a crime she did not commit. Mrs. Flye, you must know that Heather is a suspect in this crime."

"My daughter did nothing to that Bobby fellow, but even if she had, he would have deserved it."

Violet sipped her coffee, attempting to gather her thoughts. "I agree with you wholeheartedly there."

"Why are you interfering then?"

"Mrs. Flye, I understand better than you can know what it is like to have someone you love suspected of murder."

"Then you'll understand that I don't wish to help you."

"Yes, of course," Violet said.

Mrs. Flye set down her teacup and then nodded at Violet. Before Mrs. Flye and Heather could make their apologies, Violet added, "It will be a shame when your daughter is arrested on suspicion of murder."

Mrs. Flye's jaw firmed. "Heather did nothing. They won't be able to prove a thing."

"Only that Bobby's sometime lover left him, returned inexplicably, and then he fell dead."

"She was only keeping her promises. Joshie and the rest of the band were counting on her. Not just Bobby."

"Of course," Violet agreed. "Of course. I'm sure that any jury will believe that a manipulated and abused young woman had reached her limit of abuse, was leaving her lover, and then decided to return to help him one final time."

Mrs. Flye swallowed. "Bobby wasn't the only person in that band. He wasn't the only person who was counting on Heather."

"No," Violet agreed. "There was Joshie Mortar. The very man who introduced Heather to the criminal Bobby and changed the fate of Heather's life."

"It wasn't Joshie's fault," Heather said, suddenly. "He tried again and again to get me to go home. He swore Mama and Daddy would forgive me. If he didn't talk about it so much, I wouldn't have had the courage."

Violet sipped her coffee, letting her doubt fill her expression before she spoke again. "I'm sure the jury will believe you." The doubt flooded Violet's tone and Heather flushed.

"It is true. Joshie is a friend, and I couldn't leave him like that. He needed the money for playing that night."

"His father is rich."

"He wasn't taking money from his father." Heather's voice cracked.

"The problem isn't convincing me," Violet told Heather flatly. "It's convincing the jury. A rich boy who won't take money from his father out of pride. A girl who returns to help that rich boy avoid asking for help after the same fellow convinced her to go home to escape a manipulating drug user boyfriend."

"It isn't the same," Heather said. "Joshie is brilliant. He'd die in a barrister's office."

Violet lifted a brow and then glanced at Rita, whose expression was equally mocking.

"I got there just before we were supposed to start playing," Heather said suddenly.

"Don't speak of it," Mrs. Flye said. "If you do what Sally said and you can keep quiet, they won't have anything to go on."

"Sally?" Violet demanded.

"Henry said it," Heather told Violet. "Sally just brought the message."

Violet scoffed.

"Joshie agrees. He said that as long as we stand together, they can't convict any of us of anything other than being there when Bobby collapsed. He was a criminal who was stabbed by one of the people he associated with."

Violet laughed. "Bobby was a conman who persuaded women to give him money while he ran underground jazz clubs that specialized in making little rich girls and boys feel daring."

Heather blushed.

"I heard him say he loved you."

Heather's gaze darted to Violet.

Mrs. Flye snorted. "That wasn't love."

"It felt like love to Heather," Violet said, and watched the girl flush. It was enough to convince Violet that Heather was one of those girls who focused on the good times. She let the bad times go and focused on the fun, the love, the happiness. Violet didn't believe that Bobby truly loved Heather—or anyone—but women didn't leave him. He left them.

"He said he wanted to marry you," Violet told Heather.

She shook her head, tears welling in her eyes.

"He said he loved you and you left him. He died lying to protect someone. I think it was you."

"No! No, it wasn't."

"Then why are you protecting the person who killed him?"

"I'm not!"

"That's enough, Heather."

"No." Heather spun on her mother. "No! I didn't kill Bobby, and I don't believe Joshie did either. It was Martha or Sally or Henry. Lady Violet is right. I won't protect his killer."

"Heather!" Mrs. Flye shouted. "Stop this!"

"Mrs. Flye," Violet snapped. "We aren't talking about her family. Or good friends. We're talking about a group of people pulled together by the charisma of a dead man. With each day that passes, they're all wondering who is going to cave first."

Mrs. Flye bit her bottom lip, crossing her arms over her chest.

"What is going to happen is that Detective Clarkson—who is *one of Scotland Yard's very best*—will find the murder weapon or something nefarious about one of the others. By stonewalling the detectives, you all are making it seem as though you either worked together to kill him or you're working together to protect the killer. Either way, you're helping a killer."

"You should understand as well," Rita said, "Jack Wakefield and Hamilton Barnes are involved in this case. Along with Detective Clarkson, you have three of the very best that *England* has to offer discovering the truth. It *will out.* Trust Violet to help you, and she can persuade both Barnes and Wakefield to move past your interference. There is perhaps no one who can help you as Vi can."

"Why would she believe me?" Heather asked. "Why me over Joshie or Henry or Sally?"

"You didn't kill him," Violet said. "It's obvious that it was Sally or it was you."

Rita choked and Jack shifted without saying a word. Lila and Denny both glanced at each other and then Denny giggled low, muffling it with his hand over his mouth.

Heather flushed. "I don't know who killed him, but it *wasn't* me."

"Yes, you do know," Violet replied. "You're simply trying not to think about it."

Heather shook her head again.

Violet stood and crossed to the chalkboard. "Whoever stabbed Bobby did it because they snapped in fury." She pointed to Henry's name. "There's no suggestion that Henry was emotionally involved enough to become furious."

"Why does that mean it was Sally?" Denny asked. "Or Heather?"

Violet glanced at Denny and then pointed to the next

name. "Joshie doesn't love Heather enough to kill for her. You finding your way home was all Joshie wanted. As far as he was concerned, the moment you returned to your parents, he was absolved. He's too obsessed with his music to worry about anything else."

"What about Martha?" Mrs. Flye demanded.

"Martha was playing with the idea that sweat and grit were valuable. The truth is, Martha has been biding her time for a rich man to spoil her. She didn't love Bobby. She loved the idea of him being obsessed with her. She *is* an idiot," Violet told Heather and Mrs. Flye, "but Martha is too spoiled and too self-obsessed to love anyone but herself."

Martha gasped.

Violet ignored Martha to point to Sally's name. "Sally, however, loved Bobby. She stood by him, even after she heard him say he loved you. She heard him say he wanted to marry you. I don't know whether she stabbed him in the dark, when the lights in the hall were out, or whether she stabbed him after he slapped her and got her dismissed from her only legitimate position that didn't depend on him. Maybe she stabbed him when she saw you returned, but she is the only one of you who has a motive that I can believe. Outside of yourself, of course."

"I don't know who stabbed him, but Sally wasn't herself," Heather said suddenly. With that, the alliance was broken. Violet glanced at Jack and he shook his head just slightly enough to encourage Vi to keep going.

"Of course she wasn't," Vi agreed. "She'd either stabbed Bobby, and he kept walking around, or she was realizing he'd never love her and all her devotion was for naught."

"I can get her here!" Heather said. "I can get her here."

"Why don't we get them all here," Violet said. "You may use our telephone or our servants if they're not reachable by telephone. Send them notes, whatever you need to do. Explain that you're telling everything to the detectives tonight. You can't lie anymore. Tell them to be here by 9:00 p.m."

CHAPTER SIXTEEN

"*W*ell," Detective Clarkson said as he walked through the parlor door, "I'm here. Who is the killer?"

Violet considered not answering, but she glanced at Ham instead. He hadn't even been paying attention. He was staring at Rita's feet as if that were somehow less disturbing than staring at her face.

"Well?" Clarkson demanded.

Ham snorted and looked up. "Stow it, Clarkson. Sit down, be unobtrusive, and take notes."

Clarkson's jaw dropped open.

"Siam?" Ham demanded suddenly. "Siam?"

Rita glanced up at him and shrugged. "Sure. Why not?"

That question was just loaded enough that Violet winced, but Ham—the fool—didn't realize the dare in the question. For the love of all that was holy, Violet wanted to slap Detective Hamilton Barnes, the too-observant, too-aware detective, in the back of the head and knock some sense into him.

Violet looked at Jack and he shook his head. *Why not?* she demanded silently, but Jack's expression didn't change.

"By Jove!" Violet said, standing. "I need a cocktail."

"Victor left this morning," Jack told her.

"Yes," she snapped. "I know. I believe I can figure out how to slosh some gin and tonic over ice."

She crossed to the bar, stared at the bottle, and then poured herself her favorite ginger wine instead. Sipping at it, she waited in the chair next to Jack and remained quiet as the guests arrived.

When everyone had gathered, Violet waited long enough for people to start shifting in their seats before she stood. She crossed her fingers that her performance would work.

She glanced around the room and found her private detective, John Smith, as well as Denny, Lila, Jack, Detective Clarkson, Rita, and Ham. At the door to the room were two uniformed officers, and lined up in a row, so they couldn't see each other's faces, were the suspects. Henry, Sally, Joshie, Martha, and Heather. Heather's parents had accompanied her, as had Joshie's father.

"Let me speak first to those who are here out of the kindness of my heart," Violet said to Heather's parents and Mr. Mortar, Joshie's father. "If you interfere, you will be escorted from the room and refused entrance. Do you understand?"

"This is very irregular," Mr. Mortar said.

"Too true," Violet said. "Don't speak again or your removal will occur now."

To the others, she walked in front of them and then said,

"We already know you have conspired to remain silent on the death of Bobby. A conspiracy of fools."

Sally glanced at Joshie, whose jaw flexed but he said nothing.

"What you don't know," Violet added, "is that in leaving Martha both out of your conspiracy and making her a suspect with you, you have pulled in myself and my resource. May I present to you, Detective John Smith. One of London's foremost private investigators," Violet lied—more like most disreputable. "Terrible things have been uncovered about each of you."

They hadn't had time for that really, but Violet had little doubt they all had secrets.

"Things you would prefer to remain silent," she continued. "What confuses all of us is how a group of people who do not like each other and do not trust each other and are not loyal to each other would help to cover up a murder."

"We didn't do that," Henry said. "Not talking to the Yard is nothing more than protecting ourselves. Bobby was probably stabbed by some homeless beggar, and those fellows are too hard to track."

"Please," Violet scoffed. "Bobby was stabbed by one of *you*. Perhaps you, Henry, because he was keeping drugs from you or because your debts are sky-high. So high, in fact, that you'll be the homeless beggar soon."

Henry flushed. "That's not true."

"It is now," Violet countered. "Bobby's little arrangement with the rich idiots who wanted to feel daring won't work for you. He was charismatic. He made you feel like you were his best friend. He made Joshie—who was far too talented for these shenanigans—feel on the edge of breaking through the ruckus into something amazing."

Joshie flushed.

"He made Heather believe that only he would ever love her and that her parents would never take her back. He made Sally believe that he was just fooling around with the other girls and that Martha—and *all those before Martha* —were just about money and connections."

Sally sniffed and a tear rolled down her face. Violet stared at her and then turned to Martha. "I think we can all agree that Martha is stupid."

Martha's jaw snapped shut and her fists clenched, but she said nothing.

"She enjoyed the way Bobby made her feel. She enjoyed the effect of Bobby on her family. He wasn't so much a love as a beloved way to disturb Lila and Denny who—happily— have enough ready money to come buy over-priced cocktails and drag their unwitting but wealthy friends behind them."

"So?" Sally snapped. "She probably killed Bobby when she realized he was playing games with her."

"Maybe," Violet said. "Except she didn't. You and I know both know that."

"I don't know nothing."

Violet certainly hoped that was true. She walked through the way that Heather had left Bobby, returning only because she wanted to help Joshie, who had helped Heather return to her parents. She broke down how Joshie didn't have a motive. How Henry's fate only became uncertain *with* Bobby's death and it was in his best interest to keep Bobby alive, and then Violet turned back to Sally.

"Hasn't this been fun?"

"You're mad," Sally declared.

"What's so much fun is that we all know you stabbed Bobby."

"You don't know any such thing."

"You broke the light in the hall at the tango club," Violet said. "When you realized Bobby really was going to marry Heather. Heather! She'd gone home; she'd left him like so many others had before, but suddenly he cared."

Sally's jaw firmed and her cold eyes fixed on Violet. It was all a gamble.

"It must have been terrifying to see him leave the back room after you stabbed him," Violet told Sally. "How long did it take before you realized it was the drugs masking what you'd done?"

"I don't know what you're talking about."

"And you just kept going, didn't you?"

"Why are you picking on me?"

"Heather didn't kill him. She was leaving him. Joshie didn't kill him. He doesn't have a motive. Henry didn't kill him. Henry needed Bobby alive. Martha didn't do it. She's too spoiled to think of anyone but herself. She'd have told herself a fairytale that his enterprise would fall apart without her, and she'd have flit off on some adventure."

"You're mad, *and* you can't prove anything." Sally's gaze met Violet's, and the cold, hard woman's lips twitched with a smile.

"Of course, *I can't*. That's Scotland Yard's job. Now that they know it was you, they're just back tracking. They'll find the weapon. Did you hide it in your room?" Violet asked. "They're looking now."

"Sal," Henry said, staring at her, "you were the one who said we should hold mum."

"Shut up, Henry."

"I mentioned it to Joshie, and he said it couldn't hurt anything."

"Joshie, you fool," his father groaned. "Bloody hell, boy."

Joshie flushed. "I took the idea to Heather. I thought it was her. I thought Heather was getting rid of him in her life."

"She didn't need to kill him to do that," Violet said. "Idiot," she added. "Sally, however, Sally the loyal dog finally turned on her master when she realized he was leaving her behind. Did he tell you how he knew Heather was the only child of Mr. and Mrs. Flye? Did he expect a big inheritance?"

"You don't know anything." Sally glared at her.

Violet glanced at the detective, John Smith who nodded.

"You stabbed him in the tango club. Once I knew that," John Smith lied, "finding the weapon took me four minutes."

Sally's gaze jerked to the private detective.

"Really, my girl," he said, "you aren't as clever as you think."

"My god, Sal," Henry said, "I thought you loved Bobby."

CHAPTER SEVENTEEN

*V*iolet didn't think it was going to work, but Heather stepped in. "You thought he would love you? He told me how you followed him around like a lost puppy." Heather's mocking laugh was the final straw.

Sally's cold face broke with fury, and she dove at Heather. "You didn't love him. I loved him. He thought he could leave me for you? The spoiled little girl who wanted her mommy? No! Never!"

Heather laughed even as she tried to fight off Sally. "I think you mean the girl who slaved for nothing. For scraps of attention from a man who would have *never* loved her. He only wanted what he couldn't have. He could always have you, couldn't he? Dog!"

Violet stepped back as Jack pulled Sally off of Heather. Lila gasped at the claw marks on Heather's face, but Violet hardly felt the idiot girl deserved to get off scot-free.

Sally snarled and tried to lunge again, but it was useless against Jack's strength.

"And that," Violet told Detective Clarkson, "is how gossip solves murders."

"Gossip and being a girl," Rita added, hooking her arm through Violet's. "They never see you coming."

"And they're entirely unprepared for your lies," Ham said. "The idiots came and participated instead of staying home and staying mum. All Sally had to do was keep her mouth shut."

"Now you know that the weapon is findable, however," Violet said, lifting a brow at Detective Clarkson. "You probably should locate it."

He flushed and then followed Jack, still holding Sally, out of the parlor.

"Will you get rid of these people?" Violet asked Lila. "I'm supposed to have tea with my stepmother tomorrow. All evidence that I've been involved in another case has to be removed."

Violet escaped during the ruckus and found her way to her boudoir. Maybe, she thought, I'll be able to sleep tonight without any dreams. She picked up a sheet of paper and considered putting it into her typewriter when there was a knock at the door.

Vi glanced up and found Rita.

"I'm leaving tomorrow."

Violet stared, taking particular note of the dark circles under Rita's eyes.

"Falling in love is painful," Violet told her.

Rita's mouth snapped shut.

"You weren't here to watch me and Jack, but it wasn't easy."

Rita said nothing.

"It might help you to know that distance was one of the reasons we realized we were in love."

"He doesn't want to be the next detective who marries some rich girl for her money. He thinks he's too old for me. He thinks I can do better."

"There isn't better than Ham," Violet said.

Rita laughed bitterly. "Yes, I know."

"Men," Violet huffed. "They think they're so smart and they're blinded by their pride."

"I don't want to stay here heart-broken and longing."

"Don't get kidnapped."

Rita rolled her eyes.

"I'll take care of Ham," Violet told her.

Rita's gaze darted to Violet and then she crossed to kiss Violet on the cheek. "I don't know how you became family, but you did."

"We were always meant to be family," Violet told her. "We fell in love with men who are brothers in their souls. He's yours, Rita. He just needs to twist and churn in agony until his pride is worn down by his heart. I'll make sure he suffers terribly."

"Would you?"

Violet cupped Rita's cheek and placed a kiss on her forehead. "It's what sisters do."

The END

Hullo, my friends, I have so much gratitude for you reading my books. Almost as wonderful as giving me a chance are reviews, and indie folks, like myself, need them desperately! If you wouldn't mind, I would be so grateful for a review.

The sequel to this book, Murder By Chocolate, is available for preorder now.

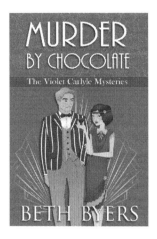

July 1925

Lady Violet is Mrs. Wakefield now, and she's settled rather comfortably into her life. During a trip to her country house, she meets a chocolate artisan, she decides that nothing else will suit than an evening at home—with chocolate—as a married woman.

When she invites her friends to her house, she little expects her home to be christened not by chocolate but by murder. Yet again, Vi, Jack, and friends are dragged into a murder investigation. Just who would commit the crime of poisoning chocolate? And why?

Order Here.

If you enjoy mysteries with a historical twist, scroll to the end for a sample of my new mystery series, The Poison Ink Mysteries. The first book, Death by The Book, is available now.

Inspired by classic fiction and Miss Buncle's Book. Death by the Book questions what happens when you throw a murder into idyllic small town England.

July 1936

When Georgette Dorothy Marsh's dividends fall along with the banks, she decides to write a book. Her only hope is to bring her account out of overdraft and possibly buy some hens. The problem is that she has so little imagination she uses her neighbors for inspiration.

She little expects anyone to realize what she's done. So when *Chronicles of Harper's Bend* becomes a bestseller, her neighbors are questing to find out just who this "Joe Johns" is and punish him.

Things escalate beyond what anyone would imagine when one of her prominent characters turns up dead. It seems that the fictional end Georgette had written for the character spurred a real-life murder. Now to find the killer before it is discovered who the author is and she becomes the next victim.

Order Here.

If you want book updates, notice of new releases, and random comments, you could follow me on Facebook. Coming soon, you'll see a new co-written mystery series as well as 1920s paranormal series. Cover reveals, sneak peeks, and release dates are all available through Facebook updates.

ALSO BY BETH BYERS

The Violet Carlyle Cozy Historical Mysteries

Murder & the Heir

Murder at Kennington House

Murder at the Folly

A Merry Little Murder

New Year's Madness: A Short Story Anthology

Valentine's Madness: A Short Story Anthology

Murder Among the Roses

Murder in the Shallows

Gin & Murder

Obsidian Murder

Murder at the Ladies Club

Weddings Vows & Murder

A Jazzy Little Murder

Murder by Chocolate

A Friendly Little Murder

Murder by the Sea

The Poison Ink Mysteries

Death By the Book

Death Witnessed

Death by Blackmail (available for preorder)

Death Misconstrued (available for preorder)

Deathly Ever After

The 2nd Chance Diner Mysteries*

(This Series is Completed.)

Spaghetti, Meatballs, & Murder

Cookies & Catastrophe

Poison & Pie

Double Mocha Murder

Cinnamon Rolls & Cyanide

Tea & Temptation

Donuts & Danger

Scones & Scandal

Lemonade & Loathing

Wedding Cake & Woe

Honeymoons & Honeydew

The Pumpkin Problem

DEATH BY THE BOOK PREVIEW

Chapter One

*G*EORGETTE MARSH

Georgette Dorothy Marsh stared at the statement from her bank with a dawning horror. The dividends had been falling, but this...this wasn't livable. She bit down on the inside of her lip and swallowed frantically. *What was she going to do?* Tears were burning in the back of her eyes, and her heart was racing frantically.

There wasn't enough for—for—anything. Not for cream for her tea or resoling her shoes or firewood for the winter. Georgette glanced out the window, remembered it was spring, and realized that something must be done.

Something, but *what*?

"Miss?" Eunice said from the doorway, "the tea at Mrs. Wilkes is this afternoon. You asked me to remind you."

Georgette nodded, frantically trying to hide her tears from her maid, but the servant had known Georgette since the day of her birth, caring for her from her infancy to the current day.

"What has happened?"

"The...the dividends," Georgette breathed. She didn't have enough air to speak clearly. "The dividends. It's not enough."

Eunice's head cocked as she examined her mistress and then she said, "Something must be done."

"But what?" Georgette asked, biting down on her lip again. *Hard.*

❧

CHARLES AARON

"Uncle?"

Charles Aaron glanced up from the stack of papers on his desk at his nephew some weeks after Georgette Marsh had written her book in a fury of desperation. It was Robert Aaron who had discovered the book, and it was Charles Aaron who would give it life.

Robert had been working at Aaron & Luther Publishing House for a year before Georgette's book appeared in the mail, and he read the slush pile of books that were submitted by new authors before either of the partners stepped in. It was an excellent rewarding work when you found that one book that separated itself from the pile, and Robert got that thrill of excitement every time he found a book that had a touch of *something*. It was the very feeling that had Charles himself pursuing a career in publishing and eventually creating his own firm.

It didn't seem to matter that Charles had his long history

of discovering authors and their books. Familiarity had most definitely *not* led to contempt. He was, he had to admit, in love with reading—fiction especially—and the creative mind. He had learned that some of the books he found would speak only to him.

Often, however, some he loved would become best sellers. With the best sellers, Charles felt he was sharing a delightful secret with the world. There was magic in discovering a new writer. A contagious sort of magic that had infected Robert. There was nothing that Charles enjoyed more than hearing someone recommend a book he'd published to another.

"You've found something?"

Robert shrugged, but he also handed the manuscript over a smile right on the edge of his lips and shining eyes that flicked to the manuscript over and over again. "Yes, I think so." He wasn't confident enough yet to feel certain, but Charles had noticed for some time that Robert was getting closer and closer to no longer needing anyone to guide him.

"I'll look it over soon."

It was the end of the day and Charles had a headache building behind his eyes. He always did on the days when he had to deal with the bestseller Thomas Spencer. He was too successful for his own good and expected any publishing company to bend entirely to his will.

Robert watched Charles load the manuscript into his satchel, bouncing just a little before he pulled back and cleared his throat. The boy—man, Charles supposed—smoothed his suit, flashed a grin, and left the office. Leaving for the day wasn't a bad plan. He took his satchel and—as usual—had dinner at his club before retiring to a corner of the room with an overstuffed armchair, an Old-Fashioned, and his pipe.

Charles glanced around the club, noting the other regulars. Most of them were bachelors who found it easier to eat at the club than to employ a cook. Every once in a while there was a family man who'd escaped the house for an evening with the gents, but for the most part—it was bachelors like himself.

When Charles opened the neat pages of 'Joseph Jones's *The Chronicles of Harper's Bend,* he intended to read only a small portion of the book. To get a feel for what Robert had seen and perhaps determine whether it was worth a more thorough look. After a few pages, Charles decided upon just a few more. A few more pages after that, and he left his club to return home and finish the book by his own fire.

It might have been early summer, but they were also in the middle of a ferocious storm. Charles preferred the crackle of fire wherever possible when he read, as well as a good cup of tea. There was no question that the book was well done. There was no question that Charles would be contacting the author and making an offer on the book. *The Chronicles of Harper's Bend* was, in fact, so captivating in its honesty, he couldn't quite decide whether this author loved the small towns of England or despised them. He rather felt it might be both.

Either way, it was quietly sarcastic and so true to the little village that raised Charles Aaron that he felt he might turn the page and discover the old woman who'd lived next door to his parents or the vicar of the church he'd attended as a boy. Charles felt as though he knew the people stepping off the pages.

Yes, Charles thought, yes. This one, he thought, *this* would be a best seller. Charles could feel it in his bones. He tapped out his pipe into the ashtray. This would be one of those books he looked back on with pride at having been the first to know that this book was the next big thing. Despite the lateness of the hour, Charles approached his bedroom with an energized delight. A letter would be going out in the morning.

∽

GEORGETTE MARSH

It was on the very night that Charles read the *Chronicles* that Miss Georgette Dorothy Marsh paced, once again, in front of her fireplace. The wind whipped through the town of Bard's Crook sending a flurry of leaves swirling around the graves in the small churchyard and then shooing them down to a small lane off of High Street where the elderly Mrs. Henry Parker had been awake for some time. She had woken worried over her granddaughter who was recovering too slowly from the measles.

The wind rushed through the cottages at the end of the lane, causing the gate at the Wilkes house to rattle. Dr. Wilkes and his wife were curled up together in their bed sharing warmth in the face of the changing weather. A couple much in love, snuggling into their beds on a windy evening was a joy for them both.

The leaves settled into a pile in the corner of the picket fence right at the very last cottage on that lane of Miss Georgette Dorothy Marsh. Throughout most of Bard's Crook, people were sleeping. Their hot water bottles were at the ends of their beds, their blankets were piled high, and they went to bed prepared for another day. The unseasonable chill had more than one household enjoying a warm cup of milk at bedtime, though not Miss Marsh's economizing household.

Miss Marsh, unlike the others, was not asleep. She didn't have a fire as she was quite at the end of her income and every adjustment must be made. If she were going to be honest with herself, and she very much didn't want to be— she was past the end of her income. Her account had become overdraft, her dividends had dried up, and it might be time to recognize that her last-ditch effort of writing a book about her neighbors had not been successful.

She had looked at the lives of folks like Anthony Trollope who both worked and wrote novels and Louisa May Alcott who wrote to relieve the stress of her life and to help bring in financial help. As much as Georgette loved to read, and she did, she loved the idea that somewhere out there an author was using their art to restart their lives. There was a romance to being a writer, but she wondered just how many writers were pragmatic behind the fairytales they crafted. It wasn't, Georgette thought, going to be her story like Louisa May Alcott. Georgette was going to do something else.

"Miss Georgie," Eunice said, "I can hear you. You'll catch something dreadful if you don't sleep." The sound of muttering chased Georgie, who had little doubt Eunice was complaining about catching something dreadful herself.

"I'm sorry, Eunice," Georgie called. "I—" Georgie opened the door to her bedroom and faced the woman. She had worked for Mr. and Mrs. Marsh when Georgie had been born and in all the years of loss and change, Eunice had never left Georgie. Even now when the economies made them both uncomfortable. "Perhaps—"

"It'll be all right in the end, Miss Georgie. Now to bed with you."

Georgette did not, however, go to bed. Instead, she pulled out her pen and paper and listed all of the things she might do to further economize. They had a kitchen garden already, and it provided the vast majority of what they ate. They did their own mending and did not buy new clothes. They had one goat that they milked and made their own cheese. Though Georgette had to recognize that she rather feared goats. They were, of all creatures, devils. They would just randomly knock one over.

Georgie shivered and refused to consider further goats. Perhaps she could tutor someone? She thought about those she knew and realized that no one in Bard's Crook would hire the quiet Georgette Dorothy Marsh to influence their children. The village's wallflower and cipher? Hardly a legitimate option for any caring parent. Georgette was all too aware of what her neighbors thought of her. She rose again, pacing more quietly as she considered and rejected her options.

Georgie paced until quite late and then sat down with her pen and paper and wondered if she should try again with her writing. Something else. Something with more imagination. She had started her book with fits until she'd landed on practicing writing by describing an episode of her village. It had grown into something more, something beyond Bard's Crook with just conclusions to the lives she saw around her.

When she'd started *The Chronicles of Harper's Bend,* she had been more desperate than desirous of a career in writing.

Once again, she recognized that she must do something and she wasn't well-suited to anything but writing. There were no typist jobs in Bard's Crook, no secretarial work. The time when rich men paid for companions for their wives or elderly mothers was over, and the whole of the world was struggling to survive, Georgette included.

She'd thought of going to London for work, but if she left her snug little cottage, she'd have to pay for lodging elsewhere. Georgie sighed into her palm and then went to bed. There was little else to do at that moment. Something, however, must be done.

DEATH BY THE BOOK PREVIEW

Chapter Two

*T*hree days later, the day dawned with a return to summer, and the hills were rolling out from Bard's Crook as though being whispered over by the gods themselves. It seemed all too possible that Aurora had descended from Olympus to smile on the village. Miss Marsh's solitary hen with her cold, hard eyes was click-clacking around the garden, eating her seeds, and generally disgusting the lady of the house.

Miss Marsh had woken to the sound of newspaper boy arriving, but she had dressed rather leisurely. There was little to look forward to outside of a good cup of tea, light on the sugar, and without cream. She told herself she preferred her tea without cream, but in the quiet of her bedroom, she could admit that she very much wanted cream in her tea. If Georgie could persuade a god to her door, it would be the goddess Fortuna to bless Georgie's book and provide enough ready money to afford cream and better teas. Was her life even worth living with the watered-down muck she'd been forced to drink lately?

Georgette put on her dress, which had been old when it had been given to her and was the perfect personification of dowdiness. She might also add to her dream list, enough money for a dress or two. By Jove, she thought, how wonderful would a hat be? A lovely new one? Or perhaps a coat that fit her? The list of things that needed to be replaced in her life was near endless.

She sighed into the mirror glancing over her familiar face with little emotion. She neither liked nor disliked her face. She knew her hair was pretty enough though it tended towards a frizziness she'd never learned to anticipate or tame. The color was a decent medium brown with corresponding medium brown eyes. Her skin was clear of blemishes, for which she was grateful, though she despised the freckles that sprinkled over her nose and cheeks. Her dress rose to her collar, but her freckles continued down her arms and over her chest. At least her lips were perfectly adequate, neither thin nor full, but nothing to cause a second glance. Like all of her, she thought, there was nothing to cause a second glance.

Despite her lackluster looks, she didn't despise her face. She rather liked herself. Unlike many she knew, the inside of her head was not a terrible place to be. She had no major regrets and enjoyed her own humor well enough even if she rarely bothered to share her thoughts with others.

Georgette supposed if she had been blessed with liveliness, she might be rather pretty, but she knew herself well. She was quiet. Both in her persona and voice, and she was easily ignored. It had never been something that she bemoaned. She was who she was and though very few knew her well, those who knew her liked her. Those who knew her well—the very few who could claim such a status—liked her very well.

On a morning when Georgie was not worrying over her bank account, she could be counted on entering the dining room at 9:00 a.m. On that morning, however, she was rather late. She had considered goats again as she brushed her teeth —no one else in Bard's Crook kept goats though there were several who kept cows. Those bedamned goats kept coming back to her mind, but she'd rather sell everything she owned and throw herself on the mercy of the city than keep goats. She had considered trying to sew clothing while she'd pulled on her stockings and slipped her shoes on her feet. She had considered whether she might make hats when she'd brushed her hair, and she had wondered if she might take a lodger as she'd straightened her dress and exited her bedroom.

All of her options were rejected before she reached the base of her stairs, and she entered the dining room with an edge of desperation. As she took her seat at the head of the table and added a very small amount of sugar to her weak tea, her attention was caught by the most unexpected of sights. A letter to the left of her plate. Georgette lifted it with shaking hands and read the return address. Aaron & Luther Publishing. She gasped and then slowly blew out the air.

"Be brave, dear girl," she whispered, as she cut open the envelope. "If they say no, you can always send your book to Anderson Books. Hope is not gone. Not yet."

She pulled the single sheet of paper out and wondered

if it was a good sign or a bad sign that they had not returned her book. Slowly, carefully, she unfolded the letter, her tea and toast entirely abandoned as she read the contents.

Moments later, the letter fluttered down to her plate and she sipped her scalding hot tea and didn't notice the burn.

"Is all well, Miss Georgie?" The maid was standing in the doorway. Her wrinkled face was fixated on her girl with the same tense anticipation that had Georgette reading her letter over and over while it lay open on her plate. Those dark eyes were fixated on Georgette's face with careful concern.

"I need cream, Eunice." Georgette nodded to her maid. "We're saved. They want *Chronicles*. My goodness, my *dear, wonderful* woman, see to the cream and let's stop making such weak tea until we discover the details of the fiscal benefits."

Eunice had to have been as relieved as Georgette, but the maid simply nodded stalwartly and came back into the dining room a few minutes later with a fresh pot of strong tea, a full bowl of sugar, and the cream that had been intended for supper. It was still the cheapest tea that was sold in Bard's Crook, but it was black and strong and tasted rather like nirvana on her tongue when Georgette drank it down.

"I'll go up to London tomorrow. He wants to see me in the afternoon, but he states very clearly he wants the book. We're saved."

"Don't count your chickens before they hatch, Miss Georgie."

"By Jove, we aren't just saved from a lack of cream,

Eunice. We're saved from goats! We're saved my dear. Have a seat and enjoy a cuppa yourself."

Eunice clucked and returned to the kitchen instead. They might be saved, but the drawing room still needed to be done, dinner still needed to be started, and the laundry and mending were waiting for no woman.

When Miss Marsh made her way into London the following day, she was wearing her old cloche, which was quite dingy but the best she had, a coat that was worn at the cuffs and the hem, and shoes that were just starting to have a hole worn into the bottom. Perhaps, she thought, there would even be enough to re-sole her shoes.

On the train into London from Bard's Crook, only Mr. Thornton was taking the train from the village. When he inquired after her business, she quite shocked herself when she made up a story about meeting an old Scottish school chum for tea. Mr. Thornton admitted he intended to meet with his lawyer. He was rather notorious in Bard's Crook for changing his will as often as the wind changed direction. An event he always announced with an air of doom and a frantic waggling of his eyebrows.

Mr. Thornton had married a woman from the factories who refused to acknowledge her past, and together they had three children. Those children—now adults—included two rebellious sons and one clinging daughter. He also had quite a slew of righteous nephews who deserved the acclaim they received. Whenever his wife bullied him too hard or his sons rebelled too overtly, the will altered in favor of the righteous nephews until such time as an appropriate repentance could be made.

Georgie had long since taken to watching the flip-flopping of the will with a delighted air. As far as she could tell, no one but herself enjoyed the changing of his will, but enjoying things that others didn't seem to notice had long been her fate.

The fortunate news of the inheritance situation was that Mr. Thornton's nephews were unaware of the changing of their fortunes. The clinging daughter's fortune was set in stone. She never rebelled and thus never had her fortunes reversed, but she clung rather too fiercely to be a favored inheritor.

Mr. Thornton handed Miss Marsh down from the train, offered to share a black cab, and then left her without regret when she made a weak excuse. Miss Marsh selected her own black cab, cutting into her ready money dreadfully, and hoped that whatever occurred today would restore her cash in hand.

CHARLES AARON

"Mr. Aaron," Schmidt said, "your afternoon appointment has arrived."

"Wonderful," Charles replied. "Send him in with tea, will you Schmidtty?"

"Her, sir."

"Her? Isn't my appointment with an author?" Charles felt a flash of irritation. He was very much looking forward to meeting the author of *The Chronicles of Harper's*

Bend. He had, in fact, read the book twice more since that first time.

Schmidt's lips twitched when he said, "It seems the author is a Miss Marsh."

Charles thought over the book and realized that of course Mr. Jones was a Miss Marsh. Who but a woman would realize the fierce shame of bribing one's children with candies to behave for church? Charles could almost hear the tirade of his grandmother about the lack of mothering skills in the upcoming generations.

"Well, send her in, and tea as well." Charles rubbed his hands together in glee. He did adore meeting new writers. They were never what you expected, but they all had one thing in common. Behind their dull or beautiful faces, behind their polite smiles and small talk, there were whole worlds. Characters with secrets that only the writer knew. Unnecessary histories that were cut viciously from the story and hidden away only to be known by the author.

Charles rather enjoyed asking the writers random questions about their characters' secret histories. Tell me, author, Charles would say, as they shared a cup of tea or a pipe, what does so-and-so do on Christmas morning? Or what is his/her favorite color? He loved when they answered readily, knowing that of course so-and-so woke early on Christmas morning, opened presents and had a rather spectacular full English only to sleep it off on the Chesterfield near the fire.

He loved it when they described what they ate down to the nearest detail as though the character's traditional breakfast had been made since time immemorial rather than born with a pen and hidden behind the gaze of the person with whom Charles was sharing an hour or two.

Charles had long since become inured to the varying attitudes of authors. Thomas Spencer, who had given Charles a rather terrible headache that had been cured by Miss Marsh's delightful book, wore dandified clothes and had an arrogant air. Spencer felt the cleverness of his books justified his rudeness.

On the other hand, an even more brilliant writer, Henry Moore, was a little man with a large stomach. He kept a half-dozen cats, spoiled his children terribly, and was utterly devoted to his wife. In a gathering of authors, Moore would be the most successful and the cleverest by far but be overshadowed by every other writer in attendance.

Miss Marsh, Charles saw, fell into the 'Moore' category. She seemed as timid as a newborn rabbit as she edged into his office. Her gaze flit about, taking in the stack of manuscripts, the shelf of books he'd published over the course of his career, the windows that looked onto a dingy alleyway, and the large wooden desk.

She was, he thought, a dowdy little thing. Her eyes were nice enough, but they barely met his own, and she didn't seem to know quite what to say. Her freckles seemed to be rather spectacular—if one liked freckles—but it was hard to anything with her timid movements. Especially with her face barely meeting his own. That was all right, he thought, he'd done this many times, and she was very new to the selling of a book and the signing of contracts.

"Hello," he said rather cheerily, hoping that his tone would set her at ease.

She glanced up at him and then back down, her gaze darting around his office again. Mr. Aaron wondered just what she was seeing amidst all of his things. He wouldn't be surprised to find she was noting things that the average fellow would overlook.

"Would you like tea?"

Miss Marsh nodded, and he poured her a cup to which she added a hefty amount of cream and sugar. He grinned at the sight of her milky tea and then leaned back as she slowly spun her teacup on the saucer.

"Why Joseph Jones? Why a pen name at all?"

Miss Marsh blinked rather rapidly and then admitted, "Well..." Her gaze darted to the side, and she said, "I was rather inspired by my neighbors, but I would prefer to avoid their gossip as well. Can you imagine?" A cheeky grin crossed her face for a moment, and he was entranced. "If they discovered that Antoinette Moore wrote a book?"

"Is that you?"

"Pieces of her," she admitted, and he frowned. The quiet woman in front of him certainly had the mannerisms of the character, but he couldn't quite see Miss Moore writing a book and sending it off. She was such an innocuous, almost unnecessary character in the book.

Was Miss Marsh was a literary portraitist? He grinned at the idea and wanted nothing more than to visit Harper's Bend or wherever it was that this realistic portrayal existed in real life. What he would give to have an afternoon tea with the likes of Mrs. Morton and her ilk.

Mr. Aaron glanced over Miss Marsh. Her old cloche and worn coat were not lost on him, and he supposed if he'd met her anywhere else he'd never have looked at her twice. Having read her book, however, he suddenly felt as though she were far more charming than she'd otherwise have been.

Her gaze, with ordinary medium brown eyes, seemed to

have untold depths, and her freckles seemed to be an outward indicator of a woman who could look at her village and turn it into a witty caricature, acting as a warning that this was a woman who said nothing and noticed everything.

He grinned at her. "I read your book, and I liked it."

Her eyes flashed and a bright grin crossed her face, and he realized she was a little prettier than he'd noticed. It was that shocked delight on her face that made him add, "I like it quite well indeed."

Miss Marsh clasped her hands tightly together, and Mr. Aaron did not miss how her grip camouflaged the trembling of her hands.

"Tell me about it," he said kindly. "Why did you write it? This is a portrait of your neighbors?"

It was the kindness that got Miss Marsh to open up, and then she couldn't seem to stem the tide of her thoughts; they sped out. "Well, it was my dividends you see. They've quite dried up. I was struggling before, but they'd always come in and then they didn't, and I was quite—" Miss Marsh trailed off and Mr. Aaron could imagine the situation all too easily. "at my wit's end. Only then I thought of Louisa May Alcott and the other lady writers, and I thought I might as well try as not."

The world was struggling and Miss Marsh, who may have escaped the early failing of things, had eventually succumbed as so many had. As she said, her dividends had dried up. He could imagine her lying awake worried and uncertain or perhaps pacing her home. There was something so unpretentious about her revelation that Mr. Aaron was even more charmed. She'd come to the end of things, and she'd turned that worry into the most charming of stories. Not just a charming story, but one filled with heart and delight in the little things. He liked her all the better for it.

If you enjoyed this sample, the rest of the book is available for purchase on Amazon or for free through Kindle Unlimited by clicking here.

50769205R00099

Made in the USA
Middletown, DE
27 June 2019